DEVIL'S
BUTTE

Also by Ray Hogan
in Thorndike Large Print ®

The Bloodrock Valley War
Solitude's Lawman
The Renegade Gun
The Vengeance Gun
Trouble at Tenkiller

This Large Print Book carries the
Seal of Approval of N.A.V.H.

DEVIL'S BUTTE

Ray Hogan

Thorndike Press • Thorndike, Maine

Thorndike Large Print ® Western Series.

Published in 1993 by arrangement with
Donald MacCampbell, Inc.

The tree indicium is a trademark of Thorndike Press.

The text of this Large Print edition is unabridged.
Other aspects of the book may vary from the original.

Set in 16 pt. News Plantin by Lynn M. Hathaway.

Printed in the United States on acid-free, high opacity paper. ∞

Library of Congress Cataloging in Publication Data

Hogan, Ray, 1908–
    Devil's butte / by Ray Hogan.
        p.   cm.
    ISBN 1-56054-574-7 (alk. paper : lg. print)
    1. Large type books. I. Title.
    [PS3558.O3473D4   1993]
    813'.54—dc20   93-7857

DEVIL'S
BUTTE

I

Dave Bonner shifted on his saddle and tugged at the money belt encircling his waist. The three thousand in currency and gold and silver coin he was carrying made it bulky and uncomfortable — but it had been a matter of necessity.

It had been only ten years since the fledgling territory of Arizona was carved from the whole of New Mexico, and it was yet a land of few and scattered settlements. Ocotillo Flats, from where he came, like most of those settlements boasted no bank facility; there had been no choice except to transport the money entrusted to him in cash.

Sighing, he settled back, allowing his body to roll naturally with the motion of the buckskin. It was midday and the sun lanced down from a cloudless sky with fierce intensity. He reached into a pocket and drew forth a bandanna, mopped at the sweat accumulated on his bearded face. He would be glad when night came.

He would be even happier when the job was finished and he could shed the responsibility that had been thrust upon him by the other ranchers of the Flats; they, like him, were in the painful process of building their spreads.

More cattle were needed. The primary years of preparation were behind them and they were ready now to enlarge, to increase their herds. Dave Bonner knew beef and how to buy it; he was chosen to represent them all. Cash money saved through painful scrimping over a long period of time was dug from secret hiding places and handed over to him.

"Make the best deal you can for us," he was told as he prepared to depart that morning three days gone. "We know it'll be a good one."

Dave had been on his own since early teens, knocking about from job to job, running the gauntlet of four years war and finally settling on a place of his own in Arizona. He was deeply touched by the ranchers' trust and confidence. For the first twenty years of his life he had been nothing — a nobody; now he was someone of importance and consequence, one men did not fear to trust with their life's savings and a mission that involved their very future.

Bonner had considered the assignment with a certain reluctance at the outset, not because he was afraid of failure but because of his own ranch and its need for continual attention. Neglected for even a short time, he could lose much of the progress made.

The ranchers of Ocotillo Flats had quickly put his mind at ease on that score; they would alternate in caring for his place, doing the necessary chores themselves. When he returned with the newly purchased herd he would find all things exactly to his liking.

Dave glanced ahead. The long mesa over which he was passing was beginning to fall away, sloping into a wide valley. The bright slash of a stream caught his attention, and beyond it a settlement, one of the small Mexican villages that periodically broke the monotony of the barren landscape.

There was no necessity to stop, but he decided to take advantage of the stream to fill his canteen with fresh water and allow the buckskin to slake his thirst. He was still days away from the huge Pitchfork ranch where he expected to make a deal for cattle — and the sooner he got there and completed the transaction, the better he would feel.

Pitchfork, he had learned only that preceding day, was the largest spread in New Mexico. The owner, Ed Madden, had a surplus of stock and likely would be interested in selling off part of his herd at a good price.

He reached the stream, paused briefly, and

continued on. A short time later he came abreast of the first of the low adobe huts and turned into the narrow, dusty street that wound its way between them. He saw no one, but such was not unusual at that time of day, during the worst of the heat.

He pressed on, holding the buckskin to a fast walk. Once he saw a face peering at him from a curtained window; another time a dog, lying in the thin shade of a mesquite clump, lifted his head and barked indifferently at his passage. Rounding a corner near the last of the houses he noted a building, somewhat larger than the rest, standing off to itself. A crude sign above the door bore the lettering: CANTINA CANONES. The town of Canones, however small, at least could boast of a saloon. And at the moment it was enjoying a spate of business; four horses stood, slack-hipped, at the hitchrack.

Bonner glanced at it curiously as he passed. A beer would taste good, but it would mean the loss of a half an hour, possibly more. The beer would likely be warm, anyway. Better to keep moving . . .

The shrill scream of a woman slashed through the hot silence, bringing an abrupt end to his thoughts. Pulling the buckskin to a quick halt, he turned.

II

A disheveled figure burst from the open doorway of the saloon. It was a girl — young;
perhaps eighteen or nineteen. Her dress was
torn and her black hair in wild disarray. The
skin of her face was chalk white and her dark
eyes were wide with terror.

Pausing in the ankle deep dust of the stilled,
deserted street, she looked frantically about.
Seeing Bonner, she whirled, ran to him.

"Señor! Señor!" she cried. *"Valgame — por
favor!"*

The creases in Dave Bonner's face deep-
ened. He had long observed a well grounded
rule when it came to interfering in matters
that did not concern him — and at this particular moment when he was carrying so much
cash, he found the idea particularly disagree-
able.

"Please — please!" the girl begged, now in
English. "My husband — they kill him!"

At the desperation in her tone, Dave swung
his attention again to the saloon. The horses,
all bearing trail gear, were dust-caked and
worn. Evidently they had traveled a consid-

erable distance. It would be their owners creating trouble. Drifters, possibly trail hands, stopping off in the small isolated community, having what they considered fun.

"*Señor* — for the love of God —"

Bonner's jaw hardened. A tall, lean man with sharp, deep set eyes and thick shoulders, he sat very still for a long moment as though considering, and then abruptly he cut the buckskin about and walked him quickly to a clump of gray-green Russian olive growing at the side of the cantina.

Dismounting, he looped the leathers around a thorny branch and turned for the door of the saloon. Halfway there the girl met him. He pushed her gently aside.

"Wait here," he said.

Crossing over, he stopped at the opening, caught up by a deep, pain filled groan. Whatever the riders were up to, it had gotten out of hand.

Bonner reached down and lifted the heavy Colt at his hip, allowing it to fall again into place within its oiled holster. Then, brushing his hat to the back of his head, he stepped through the doorway.

The interior of the low-ceilinged room was dark. Immediately Dave moved to one side, avoiding the silhouetting of his shape against the opening. He was aware of the immediate silence that fell as his eyes adjusted slowly to the change in light.

The crude bar was in shambles. Boards had been ripped from its front and counter surface; broken bottles littered the floor close by and the smell of spilled liquor was like a cloud of smoke. One of two tables had been overturned and smashed to kindling. The small mirror behind the bar lay in piles of jagged splinters, partly on the shelving against the wall, partly on the dirt floor.

"*Amigo* — help . . ."

Dave swung quickly to the speaker. Surprise and anger rocked through him. A slightly built young Mexican, his clothing soaked with wine and whiskey, hung like a dripping, bizarre portrait from a spike driven into the wall. His apron had been rolled into a makeshift rope under his armpits, after which he had been lifted bodily and suspended above the floor where he could view the destruction of his business.

"Sure — *amigo* — give him a hand."

At the mocking invitation, fresh anger boiled through Bonner. He moved deeper into the room. The four men were scattered. Two sat at the remaining table, legs stretched across its surface. A third sprawled on the bar, a half-empty bottle in his hand. The fourth, a redhead, was seated on one of the benches.

He was amusing himself by flipping chunks of dirt picked from the floor at the helpless Mexican.

Dave did not halt until he reached the saloon keeper. Raising his arms, he lifted the man from the spike and lowered him to solid footing. A yell went up as the redhead lunged to his feet.

"Now just a goddam minute here —"

Bonner spun, lashed out. The back of his hand caught Red across the face and sent him stumbling into the men at the table. Another shout lifted. The dark, narrow faced puncher on the bar threw aside his bottle and reached for his pistol. Bonner turned and gave him a hard, questioning look. The rider checked himself, the thought that filled his mind chilled by something in Dave's eyes.

The Mexican ducked in behind the wrecked bar and began to edge toward the door, circling wide around the four men. The redhead untangled himself, regaining his balance as his two friends — one a tall, dark man with a deep scar on his chin; the other a thick bodied blond — scrambled to their feet. Red pushed forward, head low, fists hanging at his sides.

"Who the hell you think you are, mister?"

"I'm the man who's going to make you fork over for this damage," Dave replied coolly.

"Shell out. I figure it'll come to about fifty dollars."

Red stared at him in disbelief. "Fifty dollars! The whole goddam place ain't worth that much!"

"It is now. Dig!"

"Not me!" the redhead yelled, and lunged.

Bonner dodged to the side; he caught the onrushing puncher with a down-sledging blow that drove him to his knees. The man at the bar leaned back and snatched a bottle from a shelf.

Dave spun away and seized him by one arm. He rocked forward, whirled him about and threw him into the pair now standing in front of the table. All went down in a splintering crash.

Bonner pivoted again, hearing the redhead moving in from behind. He took a sharp blow to the ribs that made him gasp and another on the back of the neck that sent him stumbling forward. Catching himself, he whirled. Red, charging in fast, went off balance, missed with his third blow. Dave halted him short with a fist to the jaw.

He could hear the others cursing and shouting as they struggled to get to their feet. They would now move in on him together; he knew he could no longer keep the argument on a purely physical basis.

15

He snapped a sharp uppercut to the redhead's jaw and caught him as he began to wilt. Hands under his armpits, he heaved the puncher at his friends and drew his pistol.

"Pull up!" he barked.

The redhead, out cold, reeled into his three companions, groaned, slid off and sank to the floor. The others stiffened. Silence, broken only by the labored breathing of Red and the measured dripping of a bottle spilling its contents somewhere behind the bar, fell over the room. Beyond the riders Dave could see the white, frightened faces of the saloon keeper and his wife, peering around the edge of the door.

The scarfaced man brushed at a shoulder. "Don't know who you are," he said in a low, furious tone. "But I'm telling you this — you bit off a helluva lot more'n you'll ever be able to chew."

"Matter of opinion," Bonner said drily. "Start laying out that cash — fifty dollars."

"Ain't about to!" the blond shot back, wagging his head. "Lousy, stinking dump like this —"

Bonner pressed off a bullet. The slug kicked dust over the puncher's feet, filling the small, heat-laden room with deafening thunder and coiling smoke.

All three men leaped back. The redhead

16

stirred and sat up, rubbing at his jaw in a dazed way as he stared around. Dave pulled the hammer of the Colt to full cock again, the spaced click of the mechanism sharp and threatening.

"I don't aim to say it again. Fifty dollars."

Scarface studied Bonner momentarily. Abruptly he shrugged and reached into his pocket. He brought out a handful of coins, tossed a gold double eagle onto the counter.

Bonner nodded. "That's a start. Now the rest of you kick in."

The others hesitated; then as the redhead pulled himself upright, they began to lay their contributions on the bar until a small pile had finally accumulated.

Dave eased nearer to the bar and flicked the coins with his glance. "Looks like enough," he said calmly. "Now head for the door."

The narrow-faced rider who had been sprawled on the counter did not turn with the others. He remained motionless, shoulders hunched forward, hands hanging loose at his sides as he watched Bonner.

Dave's lips split into a bleak smile. "Something bothering you?"

The puncher continued to stare. The blond paused, looked back. "Forget it, Charlie. Come on."

Charlie did not stir for a moment and then he shrugged, wheeled about and swaggered after his companions. Dave followed slowly, alert for any sudden moves. They reached the door.

"Don't look back," he called softly. "Just keep remembering, I'm right behind you."

Red was still unsteady on his feet. He bumped against the doorframe as he passed through and staggered to one side. The blond caught him, prevented his going down.

Dave trailed them into the hot sunlight. He took up a position, shoulders against the wall, at the front of the building. The saloon keeper and his wife had moved to the corner.

The four men crossed to their waiting horses, Red being assisted by the stocky blond. When all were mounted, Scarface twisted half about, threw his hard gaze to Dave.

"We'll be meeting again," he promised in a cold voice.

Bonner waggled the Colt suggestively. "Could be," he replied quietly. "Right now — *adios*."

III

The saloon owner and his wife came from the corner of the building and moved slowly to Dave Bonner's side. Fear still ravaged the woman's features, but sullen anger sparked the man's eyes.

"*Tejano odioso!*" he hissed and spat contemptuously.

Bonner watched the four men fade slowly into the distance. "Ever see them before?"

The Mexican shook his head. "There are many of the kind. For them it is good to catch a man alone — or his woman. It is not the first time."

Dave nodded toward the scatter of huts. "What's wrong with the rest of the village? Why didn't they help?"

"They fear. At such moments a man is alone." The Mexican turned, looked gloomily through the doorway into the saloon. "I think it would be better we live again in Mexico, become one who farms the land."

"No — Manuel!"

At the sound of his wife's stricken voice the Mexican shrugged. "There would be

19

no such days as this."

"But in Mexico there is other trouble. Bandits; the soldiers."

A few persons had begun to appear in the street, a man here, another there. All stared toward the saloon. Dave turned and looked into the direction taken by the four men. They were gone from sight. He shook his head; Canones was like a prairie dog colony, deserted when danger was near, but once the threat had disappeared, life resumed.

Bonner swung about and started for the buckskin. "Money in there on the bar," he said. "Ought to be more'n enough to cover the damage."

An apologetic smile broke across the Mexican's dark face. "*Señor* — it is my great shame! It is the manners of a donkey that I have! We stand in the hot sun while my house awaits."

"Forget it. Glad I happened along at the right time."

"It is not something that can be forgotten! Had you not passed — had you been one who would not heed the cries of a poor . . ."

"You will stay the night!" the woman broke in, laying her hand on Dave's arm. "Our house will be honored by your presence."

"No need —"

Manuel reached for the buckskin's reins. "An hour's delay will mean but little in your journey. And while you rest and eat in the coolness of my house, the horse also will rest."

Bonner gave in. There was no refusing the couple; and, as the saloonman had said, an hour would make little difference. He could make it up by traveling late. He relinquished the leathers, nodded.

"The pleasure will be mine. How are you called?" he added in Spanish.

"I am Manuel Sierra," the Mexican replied, smiling. "My wife has the name of Concetta. You speak our language?"

"Of a sort. I have worked much along the border."

"How are you called?"

"David Bonner."

Sierra bowed deeply. "My house is yours. Please go inside with my wife. I shall join you shortly."

Dave followed Concetta Sierra into the saloon. Picking their way through the wreckage, they crossed its length and entered a door that led into the living quarters in the rear. It was cool and shadowy within the adobe structure and everything was meticulously clean. They halted finally in what apparently was the parlor.

"There is comfort on the *canapé*," Concetta said, pointing to a low couch over which a bright colored *serape* had been draped. "I will

21

bring the wine and cakes."

Dave sank onto the couch and allowed his glance to roam about the room. A small wood carving of a saint stood in a deep niche in one wall, a flickering candle before it. An out-of-date calendar, preserved for the mountain scene it afforded, hung on another. The floor was hard packed, attesting to countless sprinklings and corn broom sweepings. Besides the couch, there was a squat, beautifully carved table and a cowhide chair.

Manuel, attired in fresh clothing, appeared at that moment, rubbing his hands and smiling broadly. "My woman attends you?"

Dave nodded. "Your home is one of charm and comfort. It arouses envy in my heart."

Sierra again bowed. "Have you no home — no wife?"

"A house, but there is no woman. Thus it cannot be called a home."

"A great pity," Sierra murmured. He turned as Concetta entered. She carried a wooden platter upon which were glasses, a bottle of wine and a plate of the spicy Mexican cookies known as *bizchochitos*. She set the platter on the table and stepped back. Manuel took up the bottle of blood red wine and handed it to Dave.

"That the honor bestowed upon our house may forever remain a pleasant memory," he said in flowery Spanish, "it is for our guest to fill the first glass."

Bonner soberly carried out the ritual. Lifting the glass, he said, "To the friendship and happiness of those now a part of my life."

It was late in the afternoon when Dave rode out. The time he had spent with the Sierras had been most enjoyable and he had been able to depart only after first promising to stop on his return trip.

Lifting his hand in final salute when he topped the slight rise north of the village, he looked ahead. The brown land unrolled before him in endless miles, dotted with round clumps of snakeweed, yellow-tinted creosote brush and an occasional cedar. In another day he should be reaching mountains, and while that would mean a lessening of the brutal heat, traveling would be slower.

An hour later he found himself again dropping off a long mesa into a fairly deep valley. He could see no sign of a stream or a cluster of spreading cottonwood trees that would indicate the presence of a spring, and guessed that he was in for a dry camp that night. But he was accustomed to such. A man could ride for days in the west and not encounter water. Long ago he had learned to prepare for it.

He threw a look at the lowering sun. It would be gone behind the black, ragged rim of *malpai* hills to the west very soon. He would ride late, as he had earlier decided, and make up for lost time. One thing he needn't worry about was halting for an evening meal; the light repast at the Sierras, which had begun with wine and cakes, had ended in a complete supper of *posole, tamales* covered with thick chili sauce, tender corn *tortillas* and thick Mexican chocolate.

Near midnight he halted in a narrow, bush littered coulee halfway up a long slope. There was only a thin stand of grass for the buckskin to graze on, but he, too, had fed well at the Sierras on sweet alfalfa and needed little.

Bonner was up in the saddle well before the first yellow flare of sunrise. With an early start he should reach Bent's Crossing, a settlement to the east, before dark. Perhaps he'd spend the night there, sleep in a bed for a change. It seemed like weeks since he had lain on a mattress, slept with a roof over his head.

The soft swish of a rope cutting through the quiet sent alarm racing through him. He whirled to face the sound, heard it again from a different point. Abruptly he felt a loop settle about his shoulders and struggled to shake off the coil. Another claimed him, and then a third encircled his body and drew up tight. Helpless, pinned in a web, he looked angrily around.

A rider moved from behind a clump of mesquite. It was the tall man with the scarred chin. There was no need to wonder who was at the ends of the three ropes.

They appeared one by one, coming from different directions, each maintaining hard pressure on his line. The redhead's face was swollen from the blows he had absorbed during the fight at Sierra's and there was a long welt under the eye of the man called Charlie.

"Told you we'd be meeting up again," Scarface said with a wicked grin. "Spotted you riding this way. Took a notion to wait."

Red gave his rope a vicious jerk. Dave winced as the strands bit into his arms. He returned the rider's stare.

"So?"

"Got a mite of squaring-up to do with you. Especially Red there."

The redhead laughed and yanked again on the rope. "Cut out the jawin'. Grab hold this here lasso and let me get at him."

The scarfaced man walked his horse over to Red and reached for the rope. Immediately the redhead dropped to the ground. He crossed to Bonner's side and hooked his fingers in Dave's belt.

"Off that horse," he ordered and dragged Bonner from the saddle. Unable to protect himself, Dave fell hard. Red jerked him to his feet. The other men backed their horses, tightening the lines.

"Aim to teach you it ain't healthy to go hornin' in on somebody else's business," Red said, and drove his fist into Dave's belly.

Bonner sagged as pain shot through his body. The redhead snapped his head back with a stiff blow to the jaw and batted him sideways with another to the ear. Lights popped in Dave's eyes and a loud ringing began to sound within his head. He shook himself, and tried to fight off the mist swirling through his brain. Sagging against the taut ropes, he glared at Red.

"Tell . . . Tell your friends to let go the ropes. Then we'll . . . settle this right."

"Settle it my way," Red snarled and hammered two more quick blows to Bonner's middle, finishing with a third to the chin.

Mind reeling, arms pinned to his sides, Dave Bonner sank to his knees. He was vaguely aware of the ropes cutting into his body, of being pulled upright again and again, of punishing blows driving into his body. Through it all he could hear the shouts, the cursing and the laughing of the others.

"Aim to get back that fifty dollars, too . . ."

As if from a great distance Bonner heard the words. They registered only dully on his paralyzed mind. He was again on his knees and realized the bands imprisoning his body were easing off.

He fought to rise, managed to get halfway, then fell forward, face down on the sand. Rough hands rolled him over, began to pull and tug at his clothing. That ceased.

"Gawdallmighty!" an awed voice said. "Look it here."

There was a long quiet and then another voice asked, "What about the horse?"

Dave Bonner didn't hear the answer. A boot drove into his kidneys, sent a fresh surge of pain roaring through him. After that came darkness.

IV

Dave Bonner opened his eyes to the harsh glare of the sun. He lay motionless, aware of the rising heat; of his aching body; of the dull sickness within him. As his fogged brain began to clear, he sat up painfully.

A heavy silence hung over the coulee. Still dazed, he looked about numbly, he was alone. Sudden alarm raced through him. Ignoring the pain that washed through him, he staggered to his feet. He ripped open his shirt front and groped anxiously for the money belt buckled around his waist. It was gone.

A groan slipped from his swollen lips. Then he swore deeply, grimly. Losing his share of the total was bad enough, but to lose that of the ranchers was disaster; for some it meant ruin.

Abruptly he realized something else; the outlaws had also emptied his pockets, stripped him of everything he carried, including his gun and belt. And they had taken the buckskin. He stared out across the empty land, again venting his anger and frustration in a burst of savage oaths. They had picked him

28

clean; left him stranded in a world where no man should ever be caught on foot.

Moving slowly, he climbed out of the ravine and paused on the rim. The hoof prints of the horses were faint but appeared to be striking northward. He swept the flat before him with a hard glance. There was nothing but the limitless miles. A gray haze hung upon the horizon to the west. It could be a range of mountains or a mirage. There was no indication of a settlement in any direction.

He thought of the Sierras and the village of Canones, to the south. By backtracking he could eventually reach that point. But the village was small, isolated; and he had seen no horses. He would gain nothing. To head off on a course opposite to that taken by the outlaws would put them farther beyond his reach and at that moment that was the last thing he wanted to happen. Only one thing filled Dave Bonner's mind: track down the scarfaced man and his three companions and recover the ranchers' money.

He moved out, following the shallow prints of the horses. His pace was slow and painful, his anger rising with each passing moment. Before the first hour was gone he was forced to halt and rest. The sun beat down with merciless insistence; his feet, imprisoned in boots not made for walking, felt as though they were on fire.

By noon he had removed the boots and was walking barefoot on the hot sand. Thirst had become a problem. To relieve that nagging discomfort he placed a pebble in his mouth.

Around midafternoon he lost the tracks of the horses on a gravelly slope, but it did not disturb him greatly; the men were heading north.

With darkness he reached a series of low hills and bluffs, but he had seen no indication of a settlement or even a ranch. The gray haze on the horizon had become more definite, however; he was able to make out a range of mountains. But they were in the far distance and he doubted if he could make it to them unless he found water.

Exhausted, Bonner fell asleep beside a scrub cedar halfway up the first slope. He was too worn to worry about his own desperate plight, but not too far gone to think of the outlaws. In sullen anger, he vowed his revenge. He'd find them, and when he did . . .

He woke to the blessed pattering of raindrops on his face. Sitting up, he tipped back his head and, with mouth gaped like a fish, gulped in all the moisture possible. He had nothing in which to catch a supply of the precious fluid, so was compelled to content himself with soaking in what he could.

It was only a quick passing shower, lasting only a few minutes, but when it was gone he felt much better. It was yet some time until daylight but he decided to press on. He was awake anyway and traveling would be cool. Again wearing his boots he headed on up the slope, reaching the rim just as the first flare of dawn began to spread across the eastern sky.

He found himself again on a broad plain. Except for the small dots of snakeweed, angular cholla cactus and clumps of creosote bush and mesquite, it was barren. He shook his head wearily; he had hoped to be moving into higher country, where the chances for finding a ranch or a town would be greater. Instead, he faced another desert.

He swore softly and moved on. There was nothing to do but keep going. Eventually, if he lived, he'd reach human habitation of some sort — *if he lived*. He grinned bleakly and glanced to the brightening dome overhead. No buzzards were soaring silently above yet, but they would come. The huge, ugly birds knew. Somehow, they always knew.

Bonner paused, sudden hope lifting within him in a strong surge. Beyond the rim of the plateau a thin curl of smoke was spiraling lazily upward. He felt new strength course through his tortured body. A ranch — or perhaps a settlement!

He pushed on, his steps unconsciously quickening. Within a hundred yards he was gasping for breath and he slowed his pace. It was senseless to hurry. He hadn't the strength and the smoke was miles away. Better to take it slow and get there than not live to reach it at all.

He settled down to a slow, dogged pace, resting when it became necessary, taking advantage of the occasional thin shade afforded by mesquite clumps and the few cedars available.

Late in the afternoon the mesa began to fall away into a gentle slope and walking became easier. The mountains he had noticed earlier were defined now, a long, low, ragged formation lying to his left. The smoke appeared to be rising from a point a considerable distance this side.

And then he was abruptly standing on the lip of a broad, lengthy valley. A mile ahead lay a scatter of buildings.

V

A harsh grin parted Dave Bonner's cracked lips. He'd made it. They'd left him out there on the desert to die, but he'd fooled them; he had lived to reach civilization in spite of everything.

He sank down on the hot sand to rest briefly; and then, gathering his strength, he rose and moved toward the settlement. He did not hurry, strong pride preventing him from making any display of the utter exhaustion that claimed him.

Reaching the end of the street, he halted first at the watering trough placed there for the convenience of pilgrims and had his fill. Afterwards, he scrubbed his face and neck vigorously. Then, holding himself together by sheer will, he turned toward the first building in the twin rows that lined the dusty street. That was his sole concession to the exhaustion that dragged at him.

It was a saloon, the MEXICAN HAT, according to the sign above the door. As he mounted the step to the porch, two punchers emerged. They glanced at him curiously and moved on.

Dave pushed through the doors and headed unsteadily for the bar along the opposite wall where a man in a white apron was polishing glasses. Bonner reached the counter, leaned heavily against it.

"You the owner?"

The bartender had ceased his work. His florid, round face had pulled into a deep frown. "Who're you?"

"Name's Bonner. I'm looking for the owner."

"That's me. Tom Sutton. What can I do for you?"

"Run into a bit of bad luck yesterday morning. Ambush. I lost my horse — everything else."

Sutton's features registered surprise, almost disbelief. "You been walkin' that desert for two days?"

Dave nodded. "I was headed for Bent's Crossing."

"Bent's Crossing — that's forty miles east of here! You're in Sugarite."

Bonner managed a tight grin. "It makes no difference. Glad to be anywhere after the flats." He felt his knees trembling. Turning, he crossed to the first of the tables and sank down onto a chair. "Just about run out of sand."

Sutton said, "I expect so. Hard to believe

a man could make a trip like that — bad enough with a horse," he reached for a bottle and glass. Following Bonner to the table, he poured a drink. "This ought to help a mite."

Dave tossed off the liquor. "I'm obliged — but what I'm needing now is something to eat, and a couple of favors. What I wanted to talk about."

Tom Sutton studied him quietly. "I'm listenin'."

"They cleaned me out — money belt I was carrying and a few dollars I had in my pockets."

"They?"

"Four men. I had some trouble with them in a little Mex village called Canones. They laid for me."

"Know who they are?"

Dave shook his head. "One, they called Charlie. Another was a redhead — Red. Then there was a blond and a tall one with a scar on his chin. You see a bunch like that ride in yesterday or maybe today?"

"They didn't go by here," Sutton replied. "You have much cash in that belt?"

"Around three thousand dollars — most of it somebody else's." The liquor, on an empty stomach, was hitting him hard. He felt dizzy and his tongue was thick.

"Hell of a note," he heard Sutton say.

"What d'you aim to do?"

"Hunt them down and get that money back. First off, I need some grub and a place to sleep. I'm broke. That's the favor I mentioned."

Sutton glanced toward the door. "Well, fact is, I don't go much for credit . . ."

Dave stirred, reached inside his shirt and produced a coin suspended around his neck by a cord. He handed it to the saloonman. "Something they overlooked."

Sutton examined it closely. "Mexican," he murmured. "Ain't worth much — ten, maybe twelve dollars."

"I don't want to cash it — just leave it with you as security for meals and a bed until I can get squared away."

The saloonkeeper was tracing a deep scratch on the coin with a fingernail. "How'd this happen?"

"I had it in my shirt pocket down Sonora way a couple years ago. A drunk came at me with a knife. Hadn't been for that he'd got me sure. I've been carrying it as a lucky piece ever since. Can we make a deal?"

Sutton shrugged and dropped the coin into his pocket. "Why not? There's a room in the back you can use."

He glanced up as three men entered the saloon and made their way to the opposite end of the bar. Sutton picked up the bottle of whiskey and glass, then paused. Pointing to a door in the wall beyond, he said: "That's the room. Go on in and make yourself at home. I'll bring you in a plate of grub in a couple of minutes."

Dave nodded gratefully and pulled himself to his feet. "One thing more," he said. "There law in this town? Figure I ought to make a report."

"Forget it," Sutton said. "You'd be wastin' your breath. Marshal's old, stove-in. Ain't good for nothin' except lockin' up drunks. You want to get anything done, reckon you'll have to do it yourself."

VI

Bonner was up before dawn. He was still stiff and sore and his feet pained him when he walked, but he thrust all personal discomfort aside; time was passing swiftly. With each lost hour the outlaws could be putting more distance between themselves and pursuit.

Sutton was not around when he entered the saloon, so he again made use of the horse trough. He badly needed a shave, but all such gear had been in the saddlebags on the buckskin and he disliked the idea of borrowing another man's razor. It was of no importance; he'd get by for a couple of more days.

He felt better after the dousing and turned back into the Mexican Hat. Sutton hailed him from his quarters off the rear of the saloon.

"Mornin'. Hope you got some sleep. Mighty noisy bunch here last night."

"Never heard a sound," Dave replied as he crossed over. "I was that beat, I reckon." He entered the combination kitchen, parlor and bedroom and halted.

Sutton was standing before a stove, slicing potatoes into a skillet. The saloonman ducked his head at the coffee pot.

"Grab a cup and help yourself. I'll have a bite to eat ready here in a few minutes."

Bonner filled a cracked china mug to the brim and sat down at the table. He took a deep swallow, then settled back. The potatoes began to sizzle, filling the room with an appetizing odor. Sutton began to add chunks of side meat.

"Figured out what you aim to do?"

Dave shook his head. "I've got one choice — rent me a horse and head out onto the flats, see if I can pick up a trail. There ought to be plenty of tracks."

Sutton paused. "That's what brought you here — tracks?"

"No. I did follow a trail for a spell, but I lost it in the rocks. I just stumbled onto the settlement."

The saloonman finished chunking the strips of meat. He shrugged. "Lots of territory out there, but I can't see there's much else you can do. You could get lucky."

"Something I'm going to need a lot of. Where's the nearest sheriff?"

"Bent's Crossing. Forty-fifty miles."

"I'll do my hunting in that direction; when I get there I can make a report of the robbery, if I haven't come across them. It'll be a good place to send a letter back to a friend in Ocotillo Flats, too, asking him to sell off a couple of my cows so's I can raise a little cash."

Sutton lifted the spider, scraped its contents onto two tin plates, and set them on the table. "That where you're from — Ocotillo Flats?"

Dave nodded. "Over in Arizona Territory. Soon as I get the money I'll settle with you."

"No hurry." He sat down

They ate in silence, wolfing their food as men with problems on their minds will do. When they had finished, Bonner pushed back his chair.

"I'm obliged to you for the meal. Expect I'd better be moving, however. Any chance of borrowing a gun?"

Sutton thought for a moment, then rose and went to a corner closet. He returned with a rusty old Remington pistol and a handful of cartridges, handing all to Dave.

"Only thing I got. Puncher left it here couple years ago."

Bonner hefted the weapon and examined the cylinder. It was fully loaded. Removing the shell from under the hammer, he thrust it inside his waistband.

"It'll do. Where's the nearest livery barn?"

"Only one — next corner."

Bonner rose and picked up his hat. "I'll see if I can talk the owner into lending me a horse.

If so, I'll be back late tonight, or maybe to-morrow."

Tom Sutton reached for the coffee pot and refilled his empty cup. "Henry Peel runs the stable. He's the one to talk to. Luck."

Dave wheeled and made his way to the street. He sighted the livery barn a short distance to his left and moved off down the wooden sidewalk. A few persons were about, but none gave him more than a cursory glance. He reached the broad, squat stable and turned into the runway through the double doors, both of which had been propped open.

He pulled up short, surprise rushing through him. The buckskin was standing in the first stall. He started toward the horse, then halted again as an elderly man wearing stained, faded overalls came from a room off to the side.

"Needin' somethin', mister?"

Bonner faced the man. "You Henry Peel?"

"That's me. What —"

"Where'd you get that horse?" Dave cut in, pointing at the buckskin.

Peel frowned and a trace of anger moved into his eyes. "Can't see as that's any of your business —"

"The hell it's not! That horse belongs to me. It was stolen a couple of days ago. Where'd you get him?"

Peel shrugged his thin shoulders. "Sayin' that don't mean nothin'. Take some provin' —"

"I can prove it!" Bonner snapped. His brain was moving fast. The buckskin's presence could mean only one thing — the outlaws had been in Sugarite, could possibly still be around. Tom Sutton had denied seeing four riders, but that was understandable. He could have been busy at the time they rode in.

"You got a bill of sale or somethin'?"

The stableman's question brought Bonner to the moment. "Not on me," he said. "That horse is wearing a brand on the off hip. Box B."

"Maybe you seen that yesterday or the day before."

"It was carrying an A-fork saddle. You look at the wool on the underside. My initials are there — DB."

Peel stepped into his office. He was back in a few moments. "Reckon you know what you're talkin' about. The initials is there. You want to take him out now?"

"First I'd like to know where you got him."

"He was picked up runnin' loose on the flats."

Dave Bonner's hopes fell. Evidently the outlaws had led the buckskin until they felt certain he was beyond recovery, and then released him.

Peel ducked again into his office, returning with Bonner's gear. Propping the saddle against the wall of the runway, he entered the stall and backed the buckskin out.

"Little matter of a feed bill," he said, throwing the blanket into place. "Dollar and a half."

"I'm going to be around a few days," Dave said. "Mind waiting until I'm ready to pull out before I settle up?" Peel hesitated and Bonner added, "I'm staying over at Tom Sutton's."

The stableman resumed his work. "It'll be all right, I reckon," he said grudgingly.

A thought came suddenly to Bonner. If he knew where the buckskin had been found, it could save a lot of time otherwise spent in trying to pick up the trail of the outlaws.

"Who'd you say found my horse?"

"Didn't say, but it was Cal Sackett — Ed Madden's boy."

Madden! He was the owner of Pitchfork — the ranch where he had intended to deal for cattle. Dave frowned, thinking of Peel's words.

"Madden's boy?"

"Well, he ain't actually Madden's son, but Ed raised him. Might just as well be his kin, he's that close." Finished with the buckskin, the livery stable owner stepped back and handed the reins to Bonner. "You aimin' to see Cal?"

"I figure it's a good idea. Maybe he can put me on the trail of the outlaws who ambushed me. He in town?"

"Not so far as I know," Peel said, clawing at the stubble of beard on his chin. "Expect you'll have to trot yourself out to the ranch."

Dave swung onto the saddle. "How do I get there?"

"Road forks north of town. Take the left — leads you to what folks around here call the Devil's Butte country. Ed's place is this side."

VII

The care the buckskin had received at Peel's stable had put him in fine fettle. He moved off down the street in quick, anxious steps. Bonner held the horse down until they reached the last of the buildings and then let him have his head. Immediately the buckskin broke into a fast lope. A short time later the road split. Following the stableman's directions, Dave held to the left.

It might be a long ride for nothing, he realized. Sackett could have found the buckskin miles from the trail taken by the outlaws. A wandering horse, drifting aimlessly, often covered a vast amount of territory. But it was all he had to go on; desperate, he was ready to accept any lead, however slender.

He rode steadily, taking interest in the country despite his low state of mind. Grass was good and the cattle he saw here and there were in prime condition. Evidently the valley had enjoyed a wet spring.

A covey of blue quail, drumming out almost from under the buckskin's hooves, gave him a momentary start. Smiling, he watched them soar into a sandy wash and scurry into the safety of the brush. Their flight disturbed a long-eared jackrabbit and sent him bounding off in high leaps that carried him over clumps of sage and doveweed with effortless grace.

It was excellent cattle country and it made him think of his own ranch and its many drawbacks. But there would be disadvantages here, too, he knew. Man had yet to find the perfect Eden. Perhaps his own Box B spread had inadequacies, but time would bring improvements.

The trail began to veer north and in the distance a line of blue shadowed hills were taking shape. Probably that would be where Ed Madden's Pitchfork spread lay.

He thought again of the lost money as the buckskin loped tirelessly on. What would be his next move if he learned nothing of value at Madden's? Should he return to Ocotillo Flats, tell the ranchers of the ambush and admit that he had lost all of their hard earned cash — and that the chances for its recovery were very slim? Or should he go ahead, as he had planned at first, send for money and endeavor to hunt down the thieves?

It would have been better now, he realized, if the outlaws had kept the buckskin, thus giving him something definite to pursue: four men leading a buckskin horse, possibly offering him for sale. People would remember that.

To simply look for four nameless men and with no better description than he could supply — a redhead, a blond, a thin, sharp-faced man and one with a scar on his chin — was almost a waste of time. Except for the scar, such descriptions could fit hundreds of men.

If they continued traveling as a group, it would be somewhat easier to trace them. If they separated, however, which they were likely to do with so much cash to split between them, it could take months — years — to run them down. *Admit it,* he told himself. *It's a hopeless situation.*

But Dave Bonner refused to accept that as a final conclusion.

He would simply have to act fast. If Sackett proved to be of no help, he'd double back and head for Bent's Crossing, keeping an eye open all the way across the flat for tracks. Now that he considered it the Crossing appeared to be a good bet. The outlaws had avoided Sugarite; with the money burning their pockets and undoubtedly honing to go on a wild, spending spree, they would make for the next town of any size.

Dave glanced ahead. The flat was beginning to drop into a deep, brush filled bowl that was broken by innumerable small hills and buttes. The haze of mountains he had noted while crossing the desert were distinct now; rough and craggy, with many barren peaks thrusting into the clean sky.

His eyes locked on a dark spiral of smoke twisting upward. A sigh slipped from his lips and he stirred eagerly on the saddle; that would be Pitchfork — Ed Madden's place. The ride was about over. Soon he would know what faced him.

The buckskin picked up the pace as they swung onto a good, well-marked road. Deep cut wagon wheel ruts indicated that it was the main route used by the rancher on his trips to and from town. Logic told Dave Bonner that to follow it would be taking the most direct way to the ranch.

Two riders abruptly cut into the lane ahead of him, blocked his path. Dave pulled in the startled buckskin, trying to see through the lifting dust stirred up by his horse's churning forefeet.

"Where the hell you think —" one of the pair yelled and then checked his word. "You!" he added in a surprised voice.

Bonner recognized both riders in that same instant; the blond and the narrow-faced Charlie. His hand darted to the pistol thrust under his waistband. The blond, weapon already out, fired hurriedly, missed, and wheeled away. Charlie also spun, ducked into the brush behind him.

Dave, slow with an unfamiliar weapon, leveled and pressed the trigger. The hammer thudded dully on a dead cartridge. Bonner swore harshly, tried again and got off two shots. But the outlaws had disappeared into the dense growth. Dave jammed his spurs into the buckskin and sent him plunging forward. A hard grin pulled his lips into a tight line. Maybe he wouldn't have to go to Bent's Crossing after all.

VIII

Low on the saddle, Dave veered the buckskin sharply into the brush. Ahead he caught a fleeting glimpse of the two outlaws, dodging in and out of the heavy undergrowth. He threw another shot at the nearest, the blond; the rider jerked aside as the bullet smashed into a nearby shrub and looked back over his shoulder.

Bonner felt the hot breath of a lead slug as Charlie cut down on him. Instinctively he swerved the buckskin, destroying the outlaw's hope for a second try. He pressed off an answering shot of his own and again missed. He triggered once more, heard the hammer click on the useless shell.

Allowing the buckskin to run free, he punched the empties from the old navy's cylinder and reloaded from the handful of cartridges Sutton had given him. Ready again, he looked ahead. He saw the outlaws had gained alarmingly, that both were now racing for a broken maze of low buttes and dense brush to their left.

Again spurring the buckskin, he bent low,

fought to recover the lost ground. He watched the blond glance back, the man's face strained and grim. Bonner steadied his pistol on the crook of his left arm and aimed carefully. He squeezed the trigger and saw the blond jolt, sag forward.

Charlie cast a hasty look at his companion, turned frontward and began to flog his mount for greater speed. Bonner veered toward the now-slowing horse of the blond outlaw. As he drew near the animal halted completely. Dave saw the blond look around, make an effort to dismount, fail and fall heavily.

Pulling the buckskin to a fast walk, Bonner approached cautiously. Suddenly the outlaw pulled himself to his knees. He twisted about, holding his pistol with both hands. With great effort he raised it and then, abruptly out of strength, he fell forward.

Bonner drew up alongside the man and saw that he was dead. He swung his attention to Charlie. The sharp-faced rider was drawing off rapidly, still rushing for the rough country to the west. Immediately Bonner sent the buckskin after him; the blond could wait — he was beyond the point of supplying any information and he would be going nowhere. Better to try for a live captive.

Charlie caught sight of Bonner at that moment. He drew his pistol and fired twice in quick succession. His aim was wide and Dave was unaware of the bullet's passage. He leveled his own weapon, again steadying himself with his crooked arm. He lowered the pistol; another dead man would be of no value. It would be wiser to get closer and wound the outlaw, not kill him.

Suddenly Charlie was no longer ahead. Puzzled and angry, Bonner hurried on. Shortly he reached the edge of a sharp incline. The buckskin hesitated briefly, then plunged over the rim and began a steep descent into a wide, far running dry wash. Dave saw the outlaw again; he was a good distance away and gaining.

Bonner fired a shot over the man's head, hoping to slow him down, possibly cause him to turn. The sharp-faced man only bent lower over his saddle and raced on. He appeared to be heading for a thick stand of brush that sprayed out from the shoulder of a low butte.

He would lose the outlaw there, Dave realized, unless he could overtake him before he reached the shelter of the ragged cedars and tall saltbush.

The buckskin hit the bottom of the slope and was once more on fairly stable footing. Bonner angled him toward the bluff. He could no longer see Charlie and the fear was already growing within him that he had lost the outlaw. But he kept going, urging the buckskin to do his best across the sandy wash.

He gained the fringe of the cedars and pulled up. There was no sign of the fleeing outlaw — no sound of his passage or faint dust to mark his position. Bonner spurred his horse to the slightly higher shoulder of the bluff from where he could have a better over-all view.

His glance swept the dense, five mile wide fan of brush, broken ground and scrubby trees. Nothing. Bonner swore deeply. Charlie had given him the slip, but he had not lost entirely. He still had the blond rider.

Wheeling, he cut back across the wash and returned to where the outlaw lay. Dismounting, he knelt beside the man, rolled him to his back and began to go through his pockets.

He found nothing other than a clasp knife and a few small coins. Disappointed, Dave settled back on his heels to think. The outlaw should have some of the stolen money on his person. His share would have been well over seven hundred dollars and not enough time had elapsed since the robbery for him to have spent it. Of course, he could have gotten into a poker game where the stakes were high, but the very fact that he was here in this wild, broken land would indicate that he had not as yet visited any town.

Again he checked the outlaw's body, this time examining every possible hiding place; even the inside of his boots, the sweat band of his hat and the possibility of secret pockets sewn inside his clothing. Again Dave drew a blank.

Perhaps he was carrying the money on his horse. Bonner rose quickly and caught up the outlaw's gray waiting patiently a few paces away. Removing the saddlebags, he dumped their contents on the ground. The first thing to catch his eye was his own belt and pistol. Encouraged, he probed the remainder of the items.

He found nothing else of interest; odds and ends of clothing, a folded newspaper, some tobacco, a half box of forty-five cartridges — and that was it. Either the outlaw had cached his portion of the money, or he had lost it somehow.

Bitter, Dave got to his feet and strapped on his belt and pistol. He stared off toward the butte. If only he had been able to catch Charlie, force him to talk. He was no better off now than he had been before he jumped the two outlaws.

His eyes swung back and settled on the gray horse the blond had been riding. Surprise rippled through him. The gray was wearing a Pitchfork brand on his left hip. One of Ed

Madden's horses! Did that mean the dead man worked for Madden?

It seemed highly improbable. It was more logical to assume the blond had stolen one of Pitchfork's mounts. But there was a chance — a possibility. And Dave Bonner, grasping at straws, was bypassing nothing.

Taking the gray's leathers, he led him back to where the blond lay. Freeing the rope coiled against the hull, he hoisted the outlaw's body, draped it across the saddle and made it secure.

Turning then to the buckskin, he mounted. For several moments he remained quiet on the saddle, once more staring off in the direction of the butte and the brake into which Charlie had disappeared. It would have been hopeless to try and hunt the outlaw in such a wild area. His mistake had been in slowing down, making certain the blond was finished and thereby allowing Charlie to get too long a lead. As it was, he had gained nothing.

Nothing except that the outlaw was riding one of Ed Madden's horses. Reaching out, he gathered in the gray's reins and swung back for the trail. Somehow he was not convinced the horse had been stolen.

IX

The final leg of the road leading to Madden's Pitchfork ranch followed the course of a narrow ravine. It twisted its way through a maze of shoulder high brush, lifting gradually until it finally broke out onto a fair rise.

There Bonner halted. The buildings of Pitchfork lay below. All were a clean white that glistened in the sun and he was struck by the neat orderliness of the place. Trees had been planted thickly in a broad, horseshoe pattern and the structures were nestled deep in the arch where they received not only the benefit of shade during the hot summer months, but protection from the fierce winds out of the north during winter, as well.

Flowers laid bright splashes of color along the front and sides of the main house, a low, rambling affair with a full width, screened porch. A small apple orchard growing immediately south of the building appeared well-tended and the trees were heavy with fruit.

Dave could see a few cattle in a corral beyond the house and there were horses standing at the hitchrack of what evidently was the crew's quarters. Smoke was lifting from a tin stack thrusting from the slanted roof of the kitchen at the rear of the main ranchhouse. And from the barn, some distance on to the rear, the ringing of an anvil was setting up a measured sound.

Madden had a fine place, Bonner thought, putting the buckskin into motion again; it was easy to see that he had made a success of cattle raising.

He descended the slight grade, passed under the high crosspiece of the gate and followed a curving driveway to the front of the house. As he halted at the rack a young woman, dressed in boots, corduroy riding skirt and a pale yellow shirtwaist, came out onto the porch. She pulled open the screen and paused on the step.

"Yes?"

Dave saw her eyes fix themselves upon the lifeless body of the outlaw. She frowned, brought her attention back to him.

"I'm looking for Ed Madden," he said.

Without hesitation the girl turned back into the porch and crossed to the door.

"Papa!" she called. "There's someone to see you. I — I think it's important."

Moments later the hard rap of boot heels sounded on the board floor of the porch. A man's deep voice, rough with irritation, said,

"You think it's important. What the devil's that mean?"

"See for yourself," the girl replied evenly, and again drew back the screen.

Ed Madden stepped out into the yard. He was lean, hawk-faced, somewhere in his sixties. He had tight lips and sharp eyes that appeared to disapprove of everything at which he looked. He took three steps toward Dave and hauled up short when he saw the blond outlaw's body.

"What the hell's this?"

"You're Madden, I take it," Bonner said, still on the saddle.

"I am. Who're you?"

"Name's Dave Bonner. Mind if I step down?"

"I don't give a hang what you do. All I'm interested in is Bert Skinner there —"

Bonner came off the buckskin, leaned forward and wrapped the reins around the crossbar of the rack. He motioned to the dead man.

"You know him?"

"Sure I know him. He rides for me."

Dave's eyes narrowed slightly. It wasn't a case of horse stealing after all; the blond actually worked for Pitchfork. This was putting a different look to matters.

"You know he's an outlaw?" Bonner asked, his voice stiff.

Ed Madden's face darkened. "Outlaw!" he roared. "You're loco!"

Dave shook his head. "This Skinner and three others ambushed me a few days ago. Robbed me — even took my horse and left my to fry on the desert. I managed to make it in to Sugarite."

The deep red of Madden's coloring was spreading down into his neck. His eyes had shrunk to small pockets of raging fire. "You — you accusin' me —"

"I'm not accusing you of anything," Bonner cut in. "I'm telling you Skinner was one of the bunch that bushwhacked and robbed me. They took my money belt and three thousand dollars I was carrying in it."

"Three thousand dollars!"

"Right. I was on my way here to deal with you for some stock. Most of the money belonged to friends of mine."

Madden wagged his head slowly. It was clear he believed none of it. "Something's wrong here."

"There was another man with Skinner when I ran into them on the trail. First name's Charlie —"

"Charlie Horn," Madden's daughter supplied.

The rancher whirled to her. "Keep out of this, girl!" he snarled savagely.

Dave saw her look down. "Charlie Horn," he said to break the moment. "When they opened up on me, I fired back. I managed to stop Skinner. Horn got away."

He felt the rancher's eyes drilling into him. "What're you doin' on my land, anyway? Sounds like you got caught by a couple of my riders and —"

"I rode out here to see a man named Cal Sackett."

"Cal? What's he got to do with it?"

"He found my horse after the ambush, turned him in to the livery stable in Sugarite."

"And?"

"I wanted to ask where he picked him up. I thought maybe I could get some idea where the outlaws were headed. Not much point to that now."

Madden bristled. "No? Why?"

"I found two of them here — on your land. You said Skinner worked for you? Same go for Horn?"

"He works for me," the rancher admitted sullenly. "But that don't mean nothin'. How do I know you're tellin' the truth, mister? Could be this is just some kind of a yarn you've cooked up."

"For what? Why would I —"

"That money you claim you was carryin' to buy cattle. It could be you lost it — gambled it away. Or maybe you just decided you'd salt it, then claim you got robbed. Three thousand dollars is a lot of money. I've known men who'd do a lot more for a lot less." Madden paused, thrust his head forward. "You find any of it on Skinner?"

Dave shook his head.

"Just what I figured," Madden said with satisfaction. "Ain't nothin' but a cock-and-bull story. You ain't got a leg to stand on —"

"I found my gun and belt in Skinner's saddlebags," Bonner cut in coolly, patting the weapon on his hip. He raised his hand, touched the pistol thrust inside his waistband. "This one belongs to Tom Sutton. He lent it to me because I didn't have one. Ask him about it."

"Sutton!" Madden snorted. "What good's the word of a crooked barkeep! And as far as Bert Skinner havin' your iron, he could have bought it off some drifter."

Impatience stirred Dave Bonner. Madden was as bull-headed as they came and he was wasting time.

"That's Charlie Horn comin' now," the rancher said suddenly, looking off toward the rise. "Now, I reckon we'll get the straight of this."

Bonner turned. Horn was passing under the gate, wheeling into the driveway. Dave's hand

61

dropped to the pistol at his side.

"None of that!" Madden snapped.

Bonner heard the dry, metallic click of a revolver being cocked. He glanced to the rancher and saw the leveled revolver trained upon him. He shrugged.

"See that it goes both ways," he said coldly. "If this Horn makes the wrong move —"

"He won't," Madden shot back. "But I ain't so sure about you. Melinda, take his iron."

The girl crossed to where Dave stood and lifted the Colt from its holster.

"Charlie," Madden said, looking beyond Bonner. "Glad you rode in. I got somethin' to ask you."

Horn bobbed his head. "And I sure got somethin' to tell you, Mister Madden. Only it looks like you done know about Bert."

"What about him?"

"That there saddlebum killed him — shot him right out of the saddle for no good cause. He would've got me, too —"

Anger rocked through Dave Bonner in a sudden wave. "You're a damned liar!" he yelled, and started for the rider.

"Hold it!" Madden shouted and fired into the ground at Bonner's feet.

Dave halted. The rancher stared at him coldly. "Next time you'll be gettin' what you

62

give Skinner," he warned, and turned his attention again to Charlie Horn.

"You ever seen this man before?"

Horn shook his head. "Only back there on the trail — when he jumped Bert and me."

"Claims you and Skinner and a couple others ambushed him, took a lot of money."

Horn registered pain and surprise. "Why, Mister Madden, that ain't the truth! It's just the way I told you. Me and Bert was goin' about our work, same as always, when all of a sudden this here jasper pops out'a the brush a wavin' his gun. We tried runnin' and he commenced shootin'. Bert wasn't lucky like me."

Bonner, controlling himself with difficulty, wheeled to the rancher. "The man's lying! Can't you see that? Not one word of truth in what he said!"

Ed Madden cocked his head to the side. "I figure the shoe's on the other foot. You're the one who's lyin'. You're tryin' to cover up somethin' you done."

"You're a fool if —"

"It ain't likely," the rancher said, with calm self-assurance. He motioned to Horn. "Lock him up in that old cook shack, Charlie. Soon as Cal shows up we'll take him in and charge him with murderin' Skinner."

X

The anger gripping Dave Bonner rose to a towering rage. Murder! They were accusing him of *murder!*

And they could make it stick. With Horn spouting lies as a witness and Ed Madden and all his influence to back those lies, he wouldn't stand a chance.

"Get movin'."

At Horn's gravel-voiced command, Dave reacted instantly. He whirled, caught the outlaw by the arm, and spun him full force into Ed Madden.

"What the hell —" the rancher began, and then went down under the impact of Horn's weight.

Bonner lunged forward and snatched at the pistol dropped by Madden. Dust sprayed his hand as a gunshot thundered through the confusion. Dave jerked back. Melinda Madden regarded him with steady eyes.

"Don't try it again," she said quietly, cocking the pistol.

Bonner straightened up slowly. He had forgotten the girl. He shook his head and watched as Charlie Horn and the rancher, faces flushed and angry, struggled to their feet. Two men, attracted by the gunshots, were coming around the side of the house. A Mexican woman stepped out onto the porch.

"You damned tramp!" Horn yelled unexpectedly. He swung his pistol at Bonner's head.

Dave saw the blow coming and partially blocked it with an arm. He drove his fist into Horn's belly, then felt hands grip him from behind. Charlie Horn surged in, clubbing with the revolver again. Unable to move, Bonner took the blow on the side of the head. His knees buckled; his senses wavered. As though from a distance he heard Ed Madden's voice.

"Ain't no need for that! Get him into the shack."

Dave was aware of being hauled upright; of being dragged; several faces peering at him curiously. Moments later he was in a half-dark room, sprawled full length on a dusty floor. Then a door was slamming shut somewhere behind him.

He lay motionless for a time, brain still fogged from the blow to his head. Gradually the mist began to dissolve and he rolled to his back and sat up. It was hot in the shed. A shaft of light, filled with spinning dust particles, sliced its way through the murky shadows from a solitary window in the wall opposite. He looked around slowly. The shack was empty.

With painful effort Bonner pulled himself upright. His head ached dully. Shaking off the last of the mist, he walked uncertainly to the door and tried the drop latch. It would not budge. The bar had been wedged from the outside, as he knew it would be.

Placing his eye to a crack between the boards in the wall, he looked out into the yard. Ed Madden was climbing into a buckboard. A blanket-covered shape, evidently the body of Bert Skinner, lay in the bed. Melinda Madden stood nearby. The rancher said something to her and then moved for the gate. The girl glanced toward the shed, turned, and reentered the house.

Dave shifted his position for a different view of the yard. Three riders were walking in the direction of the corral and their waiting horses. Two others stood at the corner of the bunkhouse engaged in earnest conversation. Bonner stiffened. One was Charlie Horn; the other was Red.

Surprised, Dave drew back. Three of the outlaws worked for Madden! He tried to make some sense of that: was the rancher unaware of the fact — or was he in on it? Had the mighty Pitchfork spread been built on the

66

fruits of outlawry? Dave shrugged. It was possible. It wouldn't be the first time such had happened.

And what of the fourth outlaw, the one with the scarred chin? Was he also a member of the Madden outfit? Or had he been just someone the three riders had teamed with temporarily, after a chance meeting, then had ridden on when the Pitchfork men reached home?

That sounded the most likely. The scarred man had not appeared to be an ordinary puncher; he seemed, rather, to be a cut or two above his companions.

Bonner swore harshly. His money would be on the missing outlaw, more than likely. He would have been smart enough to get it away from the others. That explained why none of the cash had been on Skinner.

He wheeled to the door, grasped the latch handle and shook it savagely. He must get out somehow, get Red and Charlie Horn alone and compel them to talk; he had to learn the identity of the fourth outlaw and his present whereabouts.

Dave began to prowl the shack, searching for something that would enable him to force the door. There was nothing, not even a small piece of lumber. He placed his shoulder to each of the structure's walls in turn, attempting to rock it loose from its foundation. The boards were buried deep in the sun baked soil and refused to jar loose.

He turned again to the crack between the planks. Red and Charlie Horn had disappeared. The yard was deserted; and the blacksmith, having abandoned his work when the fracas in front of the house had started, was again at his forge and anvil. Normalcy had reclaimed Pitchfork.

Bonner swung his attention to the window. Madden had gone. Most, if not all, of the riders would now be on the range pursuing their daily routine. Melinda, the Mexican cook and the blacksmith were on hand, but he doubted that they would notice the sound of breaking glass.

He wished he knew for certain whether Horn and Red had ridden off. If so, the chances for escape would be good. He crossed to the window, peered through the dusty glass, trying to get a better look at the yard.

He saw, first of all, the buckskin. Someone had brought him from the hitchrack in front of the house and tied him to the corner of the corral, not more than fifty yards away. Dave smiled. That solved part of the problem; if he could manage to get through the window, the buckskin would be within short range.

He reached for the sash handle and tested

it gently. The window opened with a dry squeak; it swung wide with no trouble. Exultation swept Bonner — they had forgotten to lock it! Escape would be easy.

Too easy!

Bonner's eyes narrowed as that realization came to him. Someone wanted him to make a break for freedom; someone was making it simple — leaving the window unlocked, the buckskin temptingly handy.

He stepped close to the opening and again glanced out. To his right, a few yards back of the cook shack, stood another building, a feed-barn, judging from the hay piled beside it. Directly opposite were the corrals and the waiting buckskin; open ground separated the structures from the fenced-in areas. If it were a trap and someone was hiding in the feed-barn, they would hold back until he started across the open ground. And then they would cut him down.

He would be a sitting duck for any marksman. And it could all be quickly explained; he had been shot trying to escape.

He turned his attention to the left, to the opposite direction. The main ranchhouse was on a direct line with the shack. He could see the door to the kitchen not fifty feet away.

A thought entered his mind. He could reach the buckskin by going through the house, exiting from the front door and doubling back along its south wall. In that way he would not be compelled to expose himself on the open ground to anyone lying in wait.

He stood for a minute, head down, considering the matter. There was no guarantee that a trap had been set for him if he made a direct run for the buckskin. It was entirely possible the window had been left unlocked by sheer carelessness, that no hail of bullets would halt him when he crossed into the open.

But he doubted that; someone wanted him to make a try for escape, actually wanted him dead. Most likely Horn and Red were behind it. They would fear what might come out at a murder trial and could be taking this step to prevent such. What better way to bring the matter to a close than by killing him in an attempt to flee?

Again Dave Bonner smiled. He'd play their little game, but it would be by his rules. Taking a deep breath, he hoisted himself through the window and dropped lightly to the ground.

XI

Bonner moved instantly. He would offer no stationary target to anyone watching the window and not the open ground.

In a dozen long strides he reached the corner of the kitchen, quickly gaining the door. Opening it, he slipped inside and pulled the screened panel quietly shut. Only then did he pause. Muffling his hard breathing, he listened. He was inside a small porch that led into a larger room filled with a large table and many chairs. It would be where the crew ate. A door in the far wall opened into the kitchen.

He could hear no sounds outside in the yard, but someone was moving about in the kitchen area. Pans rattled occasionally and a woman's voice was humming a low tune.

Using utmost care, he entered the dining room, crossed its width and stepped into a hallway that led deeper into the house. By pursuing it, he should reach the front entrance.

He wondered where Madden's daughter was. He had watched her go into the house

71

after the rancher had driven off. She, too, could have departed, as there were sections of the yard he had been unable to see. And the rancher's wife — he would have to be careful of her. Likely she was in one of the rooms.

Bonner moved hurriedly but quietly. He reached the end of the hall and turned left into another. Several doors opened off this corridor and at the extreme end he could see a flare of light. That was where he would find the end of the house — and freedom.

Dave paused. He needed a gun. He considered possibilities. If he could locate Madden's room, there was certain to be a weapon of some sort lying around. Finding one in the parlor was —

He froze. The door immediately to his right opened. Melinda Madden, head down, stepped into the hall. She started to turn toward the kitchen, then halted abruptly. Her face came up in startled surprise and her lips parted to voice a scream.

Bonner's hand clamped over her mouth. His arm swept about her waist, pulled her in close.

"Quiet!" he rasped in a harsh whisper.

He looked down at her. She was tense against him, her eyes bright with anger and fear.

"I'll not hurt you," he said in a low voice.

"I'm just trying to get out of here, to reach my horse. I don't aim to let them string me up for a murder I didn't do."

Melinda said something, but his palm, pressed tight upon her lips, muffled the words.

"Your pa's all wrong in the way he's got me sized up," Dave continued. "It happened just the way I said. Four men held me up. I found two of them on my way here. I saw another in the yard a few minutes ago — a redhead." He stopped, again looked at her closely. "If I take my hand away, you give me your word you won't yell?"

Melinda nodded vigorously. Bonner studied her face briefly, then lowered his arm. She pulled back from him, her eyes still angry.

"Sorry if I was a bit rough. I —"

"How'd you get out of the shack?" she asked, staring at him.

He shrugged. "Somebody was feeling kind. They left the window unlocked," he said drily. "Brought my horse around, too; put him where he'd be right handy. There anybody else in the house?"

"Only the cook."

"Your mother?"

"She's been dead for years. What's next? You taking me as your hostage?"

Dave Bonner smiled. "Do I look like the kind who'd take a woman as a hostage? All

I want is to get out of here so I can clear myself — and find that money that was taken from me."

"You think Horn and Red know where it is?"

"I'm sure of it. I've got to make them talk, but I need a gun."

Melinda looked thoughtfully toward the glare at the end of the hall. She had brown eyes and hair that matched, Dave noted, and there was a small scatter of freckles across the bridge of her nose.

"This fourth man — what did he look like?"

Dave brought his mind back to the business at hand. "Tall — dark. He had a scar on his chin. Seemed to sort of boss the bunch."

Melinda nodded. "I knew it," she murmured. "I was sure of it."

Bonner stared at her. "Sure of what?"

She turned to face him. "You've just described Cal — Cal Sackett."

"Sackett!" Bonner echoed in an incredulous voice. "Isn't he Madden's boy — sort of your brother . . ."

Melinda shook her head impatiently. "He's no relation; none at all. Pa took him to raise when we were both small. He puts on like a member of the family, and Pa treats him like one."

"But you don't feel that way."

"No. I liked Cal when we were just kids, growing up. But he's changed. He thinks Pitchfork will all be his someday."

Bonner nodded. Sackett would have a battle on his hands if he tried to take over the Madden ranch from Melinda. She was a fighter. It showed in the set of her chin, the determination in her eyes.

"Where's he now?" Dave asked. "I figure he's the answer to all my trouble."

"I don't know," she replied. "Out on the range, I suppose."

Dave Bonner was still finding it hard to believe. Sackett — as near a son as wealthy, powerful Ed Madden could have without being blood kin — involved in a common hold-up. It didn't make sense.

"There a chance you could be wrong — that it's not Sackett I'm looking for?"

"He fits your description. And more — he hangs around with Charlie Horn and the others you've named. I've seen them ride off together many times."

"Reckon there's no doubt, then."

Melinda nodded. "I knew Cal was sort of running wild. Even mentioned it to Pa. He passed it off, said Cal was just sowing his oats."

"That last crop was at my expense," Dave said wryly. "Mine and a half a dozen or so other ranchers. I've got to get that money back."

"I understand. Wish there was some way I could help."

He looked at her hopefully. "There is. Give me my gun. Then I'll find Sackett and make him talk."

Melinda frowned. "Would it do any good to search his room? Maybe the money's hid there."

"He lives here in the house?" Dave asked, his hopes rising.

"Of course," she answered, and pointed to a door in the opposite wall. "In there."

Without waiting for him, Melinda crossed, opened the door and entered. Dave followed quickly. He went immediately to a chest standing against a wall and jerked open the top drawer.

"The money's in currency and in gold and silver coins. I was carrying it in a black leather belt with brass snaps on the pockets."

The drawer contained only clothing. Bonner pushed it shut and began to dig in the one below. Behind him he could hear Melinda rummaging about a trunk.

He found nothing in the chest so turned to the closet where hung several jackets, coats, suits and other items of wearing apparel. He went methodically through all pockets, examining the linings, even feeling inside the arms of the coats. Again he drew a blank. He glanced inquiringly at Melinda, now closing the lid of the trunk. She shook her head.

Dave moved to the bed, a massive, wooden affair with carved headboard. One by one he laid the covers back. Nothing. He lifted the mattress, felt along its edges, pressed his fingers against the bulges. Shrugging, he pushed the bedding into place.

"Not here," he said wearily. "He hid it somewhere else."

There was a slight scuffling sound behind him. Dave stiffened. His hand dropped instinctively to the holster at his hip, checked when he realized it was still empty.

"Turn around," a voice commanded.

Bonner wheeled. Three men stood just inside the room: Red, his thick hand clamped over Melinda's mouth, Charlie Horn, a cocked pistol leveled and ready — and Cal Sackett.

XII

Bonner slowly raised his arms. His face was grim. "You're out of luck," he said acidly. "You cleaned me out last time."

Sackett's brows lifted. "What're you talking about?"

"You know what I'm talking about!" Dave snarled. "The three thousand dollars —"

"You shot down a Pitchfork rider," Sackett cut in. "Killed him in cold blood. We're holding you for murder; that's all I know."

Temper and frustration flared through Dave Bonner. He took a half-step forward, caught himself as the pistol in Horn's hand lifted threateningly.

Melinda, free of Red's restraint, moved to Dave's side. She faced Sackett. "You can't lie your way out of this mess, Cal," she said flatly. "He's telling the truth and I'm going to make Pa see it."

Sackett shrugged. "You never had much luck doing that before. Anyway, what's it mean to you? Since when's the high and mighty Melinda Madden gone to taking up for saddlebums?"

"When I see them getting blamed for something you've done," the girl snapped.

Cal Sackett smiled, again stirred his shoulders. He motioned to Red and Charlie Horn. "Put him back in the shed — and this time tie him up."

Red stepped to Bonner's side and grasped him by the arm. Dave shook the outlaw off and started toward the door. Instantly Horn moved in close. Bonner felt the hard, round muzzle of the man's pistol jab into his spine.

"Don't be gettin' no cute notions, cowboy," Horn said softly.

Dave entered the hall, turning left to retrace the course he had followed previously. Both Red and Charlie Horn were at his heels, crowding him hard. He could hear Sackett saying something to Melinda, but could not make out the words.

They reached the dining room, the porch, and passed on into the deserted yard. Sweat beaded Dave Bonner's forehead as, with each passing moment, he realized more fully his situation.

This time it would be different. Apparently there had been a change in plan; he was now to be bound hand and foot and then locked in the shack. No convenient opportunity for escape was to be allowed him a second time.

Likely, that had been an idea of Red and

Charlie Horn. Sackett had then arrived and decided it was smarter to hold him, let him face the charge of murder. Apparently Cal was confident that his denial of all things Bonner accused him of would be accepted — as it probably would.

If there was just some way to prove Sackett a liar. Dave Bonner's thoughts came to a full stop. Miguel Sierra! The Mexican would testify for him, identify Sackett along with Horn and Red as three of the four men who had wrecked his saloon. That would cast doubt on the veracity of Sackett and the others who claimed they had never laid eyes on Dave before.

He must somehow get word to the Sierras. Perhaps Melinda would do it for him; she had said she believed him. In that next instant he knew the idea was of no value, that the whole thing was useless. Cal Sackett would never allow Miguel Sierra to reach Sugarite and a courtroom alive; he couldn't afford to.

He moved on toward the shack, walking with slow steps. Horn's gun no longer pressed against his back, but he knew without looking the outlaw's weapon was only inches away. To break away, make a run for it, could only mean a bullet.

"Told you that little hornin' in you done at that Mex's place would cost you plenty,"

80

Red said. "Just ain't smart to go buckin' the wrong people."

"There's still a few verses to this song yet," Bonner answered.

"Far as you're concerned there ain't," Horn said. "The marshal's comin' and he does what old Ed Madden tells him."

"And Madden does what Cal Sackett tells him," Red added with a laugh. "Mister, you ain't got the chance of a snowball in hell."

Dave allowed his shoulders to sag. "Maybe so. A man never quits hoping, though." He paused, and said, "Who gets Skinner's share of the money you took off me?"

"Ain't got around to splittin' —" Red began, but Horn's hurried words cut him off.

"What money you talkin' about?"

It was Dave Bonner's turn to laugh. "What's the matter, Charlie? Sounds like you're not so sure I'm done for after all."

The shack was just ahead. Horn jabbed Bonner sharply with his pistol. "Just you keep walkin'," he said.

Dave laughed again and halted at the step. "I expect you'd be real surprised if I was to turn up with some witnesses."

"Witnesses?" Red echoed. "Where'd you get —"

"Forget it!" Horn snapped. "Dammit, Red; ain't you smart enough to see he's just jawin' us? Get inside!" he finished, giving Bonner a push.

Dave stumbled through the open doorway and instantly came alive. With a kick of his leg he slammed the door shut and lunged for the window. He went through the opening in a flat dive, hearing the yells of pain and shouts of anger erupting from Red and Charlie Horn.

He struck the ground below the window in a shower of glass and splintered wood. The buckskin was still at the post near the corral. It would be foolish — suicide — to try and reach him. There would be other horses . . .

He wheeled right and ducked behind the shack. He could hear Red and Horn scrambling to regain their footing on the opposite side. The barn was dead ahead. Two horses were standing at the rack near the wide, double doors. Not hesitating, he sprinted across the narrow strip of open ground. Reaching the rack, he jerked the reins of the nearest free and vaulted into the saddle.

A yell came from the dark interior of the barn; another listed from the far side of the shack. Dave wheeled the bay about, slammed his spurs into the big horse's flanks, and sent him plunging for the far corner of the barn.

He gained that point and cut sharp. Two quick pistol shots cracked. Dave heard the bullets thud into the wood behind him. He ducked low, pushed on.

He was safe for the moment. The broad, sprawling bulk of the barn would protect him from any more shots. And it would be a few moments before a pursuit could be organized. He had someone's horse and he now had a weapon. There was a rifle in the saddle boot.

He raised his eyes. Devil's Butte, with its shoulder of lesser formations, was only a short distance away. There should be plenty of places there in which a man could hide.

All things had happened so swiftly that there had been no time in which to formulate plans; he guessed he didn't have much choice, anyway. About all he could do would be to try and elude the pursuit that was certain to come and then lie low until dark. By then he would know what his next move should be. At the moment the important thing was to escape.

He glanced back. Three riders were streaming out from behind the barn. Bonner grinned tautly. They had gotten under way faster than he had figured.

XIII

Despite the increasing grade, the bay ran steadily, showing no sign of tiring. Bonner again looked over his shoulder. The three riders had been unable to gain to any appreciable degree. If anything, he decided, they had slightly lost ground.

He turned his attention to the trail. He had reached the first outcrop of rock and the path was narrowing and becoming even steeper. It led up the slope in what appeared to be a direct line toward the frowning, red sandstone base of the butte. Because of the tangled brush and mounds of boulders, Bonner could not tell whether it veered right or left when it reached the vertical upthrust.

He pulled the bay down to a walk. There was no sense in allowing the horse to pound away his strength on the harsh grade; he would have better use for it later. Almost at once the path began to swing right, taking a course that cut along the foot of the towering bluff.

The brush — scrubby cedars and junipers, rabbitbush, false sage, snakeweed and clumps of prickly-pear cactus — was becoming denser as the trail grew narrower. Bonner longed heartily for the leather chaps tied to the saddle of the buckskin; such would give him protection from the stiff branches and thorns that clawed at his legs during the passage.

He broke out onto a small, flinty plateau and saw that he was directly below the highest point of the bluffs — probably the area known as Devil's Butte. Halting, he turned about, listening into the fading day. Far below he heard the thud of horses starting up the trail. The riders had covered that last mile quickly, but the steep grade would slow them down now, as it had him.

He touched the bay gently with his spurs, and put him into motion. The rocky path continued, but now a change in the country was beginning to take shape. A narrow hogback was breaking away from the butte, leading off at right angles to form a canyon.

The gorge was deep; it appeared to be rough, impassable, filled with underbrush and jagged rocks that, during time gone, had broken from the higher formation and tumbled down into the depression.

A quarter hour later Dave found himself yet two-thirds of the way from the crest of the Butte with the trail still climbing. He paused again to breathe the bay and listen. A horse's metal shoe clicked hollowly against a stone; they were still coming.

Bonner moved on. Escape would lie somewhere on the summit of the cliffs, if ever he reached it. And that was a gamble he had not previously considered; the trail could wind up at a dead-end.

He pulled up short. The path forked: the right hand leading off and then down into the wild canyon formed by the hogback, while the left continued along the base of the bluff.

For a full minute Dave sat there considering his choice, then he abruptly recognized a possible solution to his immediate problem. Cutting off the main trail, he took the path leading down into the canyon for a dozen yards. Then, wheeling the bay completely around, he returned to the fork.

Allowing the horse to stamp around briefly, thus thoroughly confusing the hoofprints at the turn-off, he moved on, resuming his course toward the crest. When he had covered a distance of a hundred yards or so and was well hidden from the junction point, he halted and dismounted.

Tieing the bay securely to a twisted juniper, he moved to the edge of the canyon and worked his way to a ledge where he could watch the trail; then he settled back to wait.

The riders were not long in coming. Red was in the lead, followed by Horn and Cal

Sackett. He watched them pull up at the division, their eyes on the hard ground. After a moment Horn climbed down from his saddle and began a more close examination of the rocky soil.

Finally he arose and took a few steps along the path that sloped into the canyon. He had spotted the prints made by the bay but had not looked close enough to see the returning set.

Bonner chose a fist size rock from the ledge, and keeping well back, raised his arm and hurled the stone across the canyon. It struck with a sharp slapping noise.

Instantly Charlie Horn spun and hurried back to his horse. Red and Sackett spurred on ahead, moved past him and vanished down the trail. In moments all three had dropped from sight.

Dave sighed and got to his feet. The trick had worked. They figured him to be somewhere in the canyon below. He could now continue the climb to the crest of Devil's Butte unworried by their pressure upon his heels. By the time they discovered their error — if they did — it would be too dark to press the search.

Bonner glanced to the sky beyond the overhanging rim of the bluff. It was still filled with light, but faintly tinged now with the palest yellow. In the canyon, however, shadows were already gathering.

The bay climbed tirelessly. Dave began to feel the twinge of hunger, but put it from his mind. There would be no meal that evening for him unless there was food of some sort in the saddle bags.

Riders on the move usually carried a few provisions with them, but men working close to a ranchhouse ordinarily didn't bother; they preferred instead, to always make it in for a hot meal. He did have water. The canteen hanging from the horn was heavy, almost full.

He wondered who owned the bay. There had been two horses standing at the hitchrack near the barn. It was possible they were the ones being ridden by Red and Charlie Horn. He reached for the rifle, pulled it from its scabbard. A crude "H" had been carved into the stock. Frowning, he checked the weapon. The magazine was full. He thrust it back into the boot.

The initial could mean the gun belonged to Horn; and, logically, the bay also. He grinned at the irony of that. But he could tell more once he stopped and had a chance to go through the saddlebags. He doubted that he would find any of his money; Skinner had carried none, and judging from what Red had let slip, the cash had yet to be divided among them. He'd have his look, anyway.

Near full dark he halted at the entrance of a fairly large cave a few yards off the trail. There was still a little daylight remaining and he could continue, but the cave offered shelter and he decided to make use of it.

Turning off into the short grass, he rode to the cavern and dismounted. It was too dark inside to tell much about the chamber and he was reluctant to strike a match or build a fire, fearing the glare would be noticed by the men somewhere below in the canyon.

It didn't matter anyway. He started to loosen the saddle and slip the bridle, then thought better of it; he could be faced with sudden flight and there would be no time to throw gear back onto the bay. Accordingly, he picketed the horse where the grass was thickest and, taking the rifle, canteen and saddlebags, made his way back to the cave. Making himself comfortable on a flat rock, he upended the pouches and began to paw through their contents.

He was right about the money; there was none. But he had a bit of luck where food was concerned. He found a tin of peaches and several strips of jerky wrapped in a square of cloth. Whether it all belonged to Charlie Horn or not he could not determine — and he did not care.

Opening the peaches with his knife, he ate the thick slices and drank the juice. Then, taking a strip of the dried meat, he leaned back, placed his shoulders against the wall of the cave, and began to chew.

Night was complete and stars were beginning to show. A glare to the east indicated the coming of a bright moon and a faint breeze, cool and soft, was bringing a break in the day's strong heat.

Somewhere an owl hooted. The bay's teeth made a dull, steady grinding sound as he cropped the tough bladed grass. And then Dave Bonner heard something else — the slow, measured thud of a horse coming up the trail.

XIV

Bonner snatched up the rifle and quickly crossed to the opposite side of the cave's entrance. From there he had complete coverage of the trail where it rounded a shoulder of rock. Evidently his ruse had not delayed Sackett and his men as much as he had hoped.

A horse came into view, head down, walking slow. The bay stopped grazing and turned to stare at the newcomer. Abruptly the rider cut off the narrow path to where the bay was tethered and dismounted. Frowning, Dave stood up.

It was Melinda Madden.

Still cautious, Bonner remained within the darkness. It could be some sort of trap; he doubted the girl would be a willing party to such, knowing how she felt about Cal Sackett, but he had to be sure. He watched her tie the black she was riding alongside his mount, wheel and start hesitantly toward the cave.

"Dave . . ."

Her call was little more than a whisper. He threw a final, probing glance to the trail, assured himself that she was alone, and stepped into the open. She ran to him at once.

"You're all right!" she murmured in a thankful voice. "I was afraid they —"

"Gave them the slip," he said, moved by the relief in her tone.

She smiled and nodded. "I heard them down in the canyon."

"Did they see you?"

"I don't think so. I tried to be quiet."

He led her back to the cave. "You shouldn't have come. No need for you to get yourself mixed up in my troubles."

She made no reply, simply reached into the pocket of her brush jacket. "I thought you might need this," she said, handing him a pistol. "I didn't know you had a rifle."

"It was on the horse I grabbed," he said, checking the revolver. It was his own weapon and it was comforting to feel it in his palm again. He slid it into the holster. "I'm obliged. How'd you know I'd be here?"

"Only a guess. When you took the trail west of the ranch I knew you'd end up at Devil's Butte. It was simple to follow."

"I fooled Sackett at the fork —"

"When I heard them down there, I figured you'd sent them on a wild-goose chase. So I stayed on the main trail."

Bonner stared off toward the canyon. "They've found out it was a trick by now.

They'll be coming on this way as soon as it's light."

"Maybe sooner. Cal knows this country like the back of his hand. We played in these caves when we were kids. He'll suspect you're in one of them."

"There are more?"

"Dozens of them, higher up."

"What's on top — more bluffs?"

"A mesa, but it's pretty well chopped up by arroyos."

Bonner nodded. Then, "Can I get back to the ranch from there?"

"It's a long way around, but the trail does join one of the roads that goes west. We can follow it to our place."

He looked down at Melinda. Her face was a pale, soft oval in the half light. "We?" he echoed, then added, "This is no place for you. I won't risk your getting hurt. You start back down the trail now; I'll head on up-slope."

Melinda shook her head. "I'm going with you."

"There's a good chance there'll be shooting."

"I'm not afraid."

"Maybe so, but I won't have you hurt. I'm hoping to dodge a shootout — I'm not looking to gun any man down. But it could come to it."

"You forted yourself up in this cave."

"Only because I didn't know the country. I wasn't sure whether I'd run into a dead end. A cave seemed the best place to hole up until it got daylight."

She was silent for several moments. Finally, "What will you do when you get back to the ranch? They'll still be hunting you."

Bonner shrugged. "I haven't thought that far ahead yet. Best thing, I reckon, is try and talk to your pa; see if I can reason with him."

"He'll be hard to convince. He'll believe everything Cal tells him — and you have no proof of anything."

"I think maybe I can get some."

"Proof that he and the others robbed you?"

"Not exactly that, but I can prove that they all lied when they claimed they'd never seen me before. There's a couple — the Sierras — in a village south of here. It was because of them I had trouble with Sackett. If I can figure a way to protect them, I'll bring them here, let them testify."

Melinda nodded. "It would help. Once we convince Pa that Cal lied, I think he'd listen to all you've got to say."

Bonner looked closely at the girl, half smiling. "That *we* again."

She faced him squarely. "I'm in this with you whether you want me or not!"

Immediately his arms went about her. He drew her to him. "I want you," he said quietly. "But I don't like the idea of your being around. Sackett's playing for keeps. He can't afford to let your pa know the truth."

"I know that, and that's what makes it important. I've got something to prove, too — that Cal isn't all Pa thinks he is. I know he's just working for the day when he can take over Pitchfork — Pa willing or not."

"You think he's mixed up in other things?"

"I don't know exactly what, but I'm sure of it. He gets money — lots of it — from somewhere. He could be selling some of our beef on the side. Or maybe it's something else. And he always has a bunch of hardcases hanging around — the kind that are ready for anything."

"Seems like that alone would make your pa wonder a little."

"It has. I heard him ask Cal about it once. Cal explained it away, said every big ranch like Pitchfork had to hire men like Charlie Horn and Red — gunmen. Otherwise the small ranchers and squatters would pick the place clean. Hired hands like those keep the buzzards away; that was how he put it."

"Some truth in it," Dave admitted. "Only

95

trouble is that the hardcases end up taking over, unless you know how to handle them."

"That's what's happened to us — except that Cal, who's supposed to be one of the family, has become one of them."

"You ever try talking to your pa, let him know how you feel and what you think?"

"He's a hard man to talk to, even for me," Melinda said wearily. "Words don't mean much to him. He has to be shown — everything has to be proven. And I've never been able to do that."

Bonner allowed his arms to fall and stepped back. "Maybe this time you can," he said, smiling at her. "I'll get you back to the ranch where you'll be safe, then I'll go after the Sierras. We put one crack in the wall; I think we can pull it down easy."

"But the money you lost . . ."

"It's not lost yet. It's hid somewhere. I learned from Red that they haven't split it up yet. Sackett's smart enough to let it lay for a spell — and he'll be more careful than ever after what I told your pa. It'll still be wherever it is now when I get back."

He moved to the mouth of the cave. "We'd better start —"

A pistol blasted through the quiet. Dust and bits of shattered sandstone sprayed over Bonner's head. He jerked back into the darkness of the cave, dragged Melinda to the floor with him.

Reaching for the rifle, he levered a cartridge into the chamber. "Guess we waited too long," he murmured.

XV

Straining his eyes, Dave Bonner endeavored to locate Sackett and the men with him. They were in the thick brush beyond the shoulder of rock at the bend in the trail, he thought, but the darkness made it impossible to determine exactly.

"Crawl over close to the wall," he said, nudging Melinda gently.

Unhesitatingly she did his bidding. He was taking no chances on bullets, fired at random into the cave, striking her. Pressed close to the side she would be in little danger.

Someone moved near the bulge of sandstone. Instantly Bonner lifted the rifle, fired hastily, and rolled to where Melinda crouched. A flurry of shots echoed. Bullets dug into the loose earth where Dave had lain, thudded into the rear wall of the cave. They had targeted the flash of his rifle, as he had known they would.

When the echoes had died, he cupped his lips, shouted, "No luck, Sackett! And here's a warning — don't try getting to our horses again, unless you want to die."

"Expect it'll be you who'll do the dying." Cal Sackett's voice was harsh. "You're pinned down — good."

"Got plenty of ammunition."

"There's plenty ways to skin a snake."

"You're welcome to try 'em all. But nobody comes around the rock and lives — figure on it."

Another burst of gunshots echoed through the night. More bullets thudded into the wall, churned dust from the floor. A powdery haze began to fill the cavern, hung in choking, unmoving layers. Melinda began to cough.

"Lay flat," Bonner said. "The air will be clean close to the ground."

"Better make it easy on yourself!" Sackett's voice cut in. "Drop your guns and step out. Horn's got your horse. You can mount up and ride."

"It's a trick!" Melinda warned hurriedly. "Don't trust him."

"I don't aim to. He'd like getting me out in the open."

But it might pay to string Sackett along, get him to talk.

"You give me your word on that?" he yelled.

A small sound jerked involuntarily from Melinda's lips. He reached out, pressed her arm reassuringly.

"Sure," Cal Sackett replied. "Long as you head on out of the country. I just don't want you around Pitchfork."

"What about my money? Got to have it — pay for the cattle I was sent to buy."

There were a few moments of silence. Then, "You get it back."

Melinda stirred. Dave had felt that she believed him when he had told of the robbery, but to hear Cal Sackett admit it was no small shock to her.

"You carrying it with you?"

"Nope. It's been put in a safe place. Don't worry."

"How'll I get it, if I ride out?"

"Charlie Horn'll go with you. He knows where it is."

"Don't much trust him. Suit me better to pick it up myself."

"Ain't that easy. You coming out?"

"Thinking on it."

"Well, hurry it up. I ain't hanging around here all night."

"Neither are we," Bonner murmured. In daylight the advantage would lie with Sackett and his outlaw friends. Any move that he and Melinda made would have to be while darkness still blanketed the mountain.

"What about it, Bonner?"

"Still thinking it over. Couple of things I need to straighten out in my mind."

"Like what?"

"Melinda — for one. You agreeable to letting her pass, head back to the ranch?"

"Sure, sure."

"The hell you are!" Dave yelled, suddenly tired of the obvious lies. "You can't afford to let her live any more than you can me. But you're overlooking something, Sackett; anything happens to her, you'll have a hard time explaining it to Ed Madden."

"No sweat. I'll tell him you was holding her hostage — that you shot her when she tried to run —"

Melinda gasped. She was seeing a Cal Sackett she did not know existed. Perhaps she suspected him of many things but not of the cold-blooded ruthlessness of which she was now aware. Again he reassured her.

"Don't worry. We'll make it out of here."

"If we do," she said in a firm voice, "Pa's going to know what Cal's really like — if I have to use a gun! I'll make him listen!"

In spite of himself Dave grinned at the ferocity in her tone, and then sobered instantly. They were in a tough spot, there was no denying it. While they were inside the cave they were relatively safe, but that would soon resolve itself into a matter of who could hold out the longer. And there Sackett held the whip handle.

He could send for food, water and other necessary comforts, if need be. There were three of them; they could take turns sleeping, maintaining a constant vigilance.

Keeping low, Dave crawled to the mouth of the cave. The moon was out full strength and the ground before him was well lighted with a silver brilliance. In the welter of brush and boulders skirting the trail beyond the shoulder of rock, however, all was blackness. Somewhere in that area Sackett and his men lay hidden.

He turned his attention to the horses. They were behind the bulge of sandstone and not visible to the outlaws. A fairly large berm, created by rainwater pouring down the face of the butte, formed a ditch along which he could crawl, unnoticed, to the animals.

But then what?

The instant Melinda and he showed themselves on the trail, Sackett and the others would open fire; there was no possibility of going either up or down the path without exposing themselves.

"Bonner!"

Dave paused in his deep thinking. Sackett was growing impatient. "Yeah?"

"You got your mind made up yet?"

"Not yet."

"Going to be your last chance."

"Maybe so — but I figure we're better off in here."

"Don't be so sure."

Pulling back close to the edge of the cave's entrance, Bonner raised his rifle and took general aim at the area where he thought the men were hiding. Their answering fire should afford him a more specific clue.

He pressed off a shot. Immediately three pistols flared in the blackness. They were tightly grouped in the maze of rocks and undergrowth, just as he had thought.

Dave settled back, trying to recall exactly the lie of the ground in that particular section of the trail. The path had been narrow where it rounded the shoulder of rock; he did remember that. And the canyon wall was steep, impossible for a man to maintain balance. Such was preventing Sackett and his two men from moving up to a point where they could have direct surveillance of the cave. As it was, they had a somewhat slanting view of the cavern's mouth.

But they still controlled the open ground and the trail.

He turned back to Melinda. "You sure there's no other way out of here?"

"I'm sure. It's a small cave; shallow. It runs into the bluff for only fifteen feet or so."

"How about the roof — ceiling?"

"Solid rock; no opening of any kind."

Bonner shook his head. "Only one way out, then: through the mouth."

"It's the only way," she repeated in a hopeless tone.

He studied her face, barely visible in the shadows. "Don't give up yet. I said we'd get out of here, and we will."

"I don't see how —"

"We can reach the horses," he said, thinking aloud. "The problem's getting to the trail and out of range before they spot us."

Bonner's thoughts came to a full stop, caught up by his own words. He leaned forward slightly, hope suddenly flowing through him in a strong current.

"That's it — they can see us!" he said in a tight voice. "If they can't — if we can keep them from seeing us when we make a run for it —"

Melinda was on her knees beside him, fingers pressing hard upon his arm. "How — how can we —"

"Smoke," Dave said. "Plenty of smoke . . ."

XVI

Bonner spun to the saddlebags he had taken off the bay. Gathering up the odds and ends of clothing they had contained, he faced Melinda.

"We need wood. Collect all you can find in here," he said, dropping the clothing into a pile. "I'll see what I can find outside. Careful now; keep low."

She nodded and began to move about in the dark, groping her way along the floor. Dave, going flat on his belly, worked his way through the opening of the cave and down into the trench behind the berm. He crawled the full distance to the horses. There, hidden by the shoulder of rock, he drew himself upright.

Moving hurriedly, he took the rope from the bay's saddle, slung it over his shoulder, and then began to search about for dry limbs, twigs, leaves and other bits of inflammable trash. When he had accumulated what he could manage, he rolled it into a bundle, placed a loop of rope about it and returned to the cave, dragging it all behind him.

"I couldn't find much," Melinda said when he was inside.

Dave nodded and shook the rope free. He surveyed the pile. "We need more. I'll have to go outside again."

He swung about, pausing when he felt Melinda's fingers on his arm. Grinning at her, he said, "I'm not taking any chance. I'll be back."

"But — if they start shooting . . ."

"I'm down behind a ridge. And they can't see me when I reach the horses."

"All right, but be careful."

He started to move on, then paused again. "The rifle's there," he said, pointing to the weapon. "If they open up, better give them a couple of shots. I don't want Sackett getting suspicious."

Once more flat on the cool ground, he made his way cautiously into the open. He had to range farther for wood this time, working as near the sandstone bulge as he dared, but when he returned to the cave a quarter hour later, he had sufficient tinder to accomplish his purpose.

On his knees, he divided the wood and trash into three piles, mixing in each several pieces of the clothing he had removed from the saddlebags. That done, he then cut the rope into three pieces and tied each pile into an elongated bundle. He was careful to place the dry wood in such a manner as to permit its free burning.

Melinda watched him silently. Finally she said, "I think I know what you're up to. You're going to light those — those torches, throw them onto the trail . . ."

He nodded. "With the rags mixed in, I'm hoping they'll let off enough smoke for us to hide behind."

New hope turned her eager, anxious. "Which way do we go?"

"The breeze is coming up the canyon. Best bet is for us to keep climbing — get on the mesa."

He pulled the last rope tight, and sat back on his heels. He had left a five-foot tail hanging from each of the bundles. Once flaming, he would be unable to handle the torches; the trailing length of rope would enable him to hurl them the necessary distance.

"What can I do?" Melinda asked.

He gathered up the ends of the ropes. "Once we get to the horses —"

His words were drowned by the crash of several gunshots. Melinda, startled by the unexpected reports, uttered a low cry and threw herself against Bonner.

"Just letting us know they're still out there," Dave said, calming her. He picked up the rifle, sent two answering bullets into the brush where Sackett and the others lay.

"Bonner! You awake?"

Sackett's question was followed by a laugh. Dave made no reply.

"Bonner — you hear me? Figured to give you another chance to come out."

"Don't do me any favors," Dave yelled back. "We're sitting tight until sunup."

"Won't do you no good. Soon's it light, I aim to get you out of there, one way or another."

"Works both ways. First man tries coming around that rock's dead."

"There's other ways. Better give up — come on out."

"Forget it, Sackett!"

"Suit yourself, cowboy."

Dave remained silent at the edge of the cave's entrance, his eyes fastened to the darkness beyond the bulge of sandstone. The outlaws could be planning to make their move, but after the elapse of several minutes, during which he could detect no stirring about, he turned to Melinda.

"I'll go first, drag the bundles. Remember to keep low. Long as you're below the ridge they can't see you."

"I'm ready," she murmured.

Handing her the rifle, Dave dropped flat

and, grasping the trailing ropes, wormed his way through the opening and into the trench. Halfway he glanced back; Melinda was a dark shape behind the berm. He continued, reached the horses and got to his feet. Wheeling, he took her by the arm, helped her rise.

"Safe to move about, long as we're quiet," he said. "And stay close to the bluff." He reached into his pocket and produced several matches.

"Mount up," he directed her. "Hang onto my horse. I don't want to spook him when I start the fires. We'll have to move fast once I get things going."

Melinda turned to the horses, jerked the reins free and climbed onto her black. Dave handed the bay's leathers to her and then, dragging the bundles of faggots and cloth, moved forward along the bluff toward the sandstone shoulder.

When he had gone as far as possible, he squatted, prepared to strike a match. He wished he could get nearer the trail. Tossing the flaming packets to the point where they would be most effective would be difficult because of the bulge in the formation. But there was nothing he could do about it.

He held a match to the first of the bundles until it was burning strongly, then lit the other two. He allowed those to get well started, not wanting to chance their being blown out when hurled.

Finally satisfied, he looked to where Melinda waited with the horses. She was ready. Picking up the rope of the first bundle, now a raging torch, smoking heavily because of the cloth and green leaves he had included, he swung it vertically, like an Independence Day pinwheel, for a half a dozen revolutions, and then sent it soaring onto the trail.

A yell lifted instantly from the outlaws. Moving fast, Bonner arced the second bundle through the half-darkness, then followed it with the third.

Wheeling, he raced to Melinda and the horses and vaulted onto the bay. Spurring forward, he glanced to the shoulder of rock. The bundles had struck just beyond it. One had burst open upon impact and all were burning fiercely. Dense clouds of smoke were already hanging against the bluff.

"Let's get out of here!" Dave shouted and pointed the bay toward the trail.

They reached the narrow path together and he pulled aside, allowed the girl to forge on ahead. Behind them the yelling, interspersed with loud cursing, had increased. Dave looked back. He could see the dim figures of three men moving frantically about in the thick pall, stamping, kicking, endeavoring to kill the flames.

Drawing his pistol, he sent two bullets into the midst of the hazy confusion. Immediately the figures disappeared.

Dave grinned at Melinda. "That'll hold them for a few minutes," he said.

XVII

The moon spread a soft, silver glow over the countryside; the trail, while steep and rough, was not difficult to follow. Bonner kept Melinda ahead — there was less chance of her getting hit by a bullet if Sackett and the others pursued quickly and managed to bring themselves into firing range. Also, he wanted to be in position to return their fire.

From time to time he glanced over his shoulder. He saw no sign of the men for the first half hour and then suddenly they were there — Sackett and Charlie Horn riding abreast, Red a few paces to the rear. They were driving their mounts hard on the sharp grade in an effort to close the gap, but at the speed the horses were being pushed, they would tire quickly.

"I hear them!"

At Melinda's sudden cry, Bonner spurred the bay nearer to her. He shook his head.

"No danger," he said. "They're running their horses into the ground. They won't catch up. How far is it to the top?"

"A long way yet. The trail slants all the

way across the face of the bluffs."

Dave settled back. Their own mounts were beginning to labor and they had not been pressed at all; those of the outlaws would be starting to wilt very soon.

Again he looked back. The riders appeared farther away. He nodded to himself in satisfaction, then swung his attention to the path beyond Melinda. It leveled off slightly for a half mile's distance, then rose to top a saddle running at right angle to the bluff.

"When you reach that crest," Bonner called to the girl, "pull up. Got to breathe these horses."

She nodded her understanding and they rode on in silence. The only sound in the still, warm night was the rhythmic beat of the horses' hooves.

They gained the rise and halted. Both the bay and Melinda's black were blowing hard. Immediately Dave dismounted and wheeled to assist the girl, but she was already beside him. Together they walked to the edge of the trail and looked back. It fell away below them in an undulating, silver strip to disappear, finally, into utter darkness.

"I — I can't see them," Melinda murmured. "Do you think they've given up?"

"No such luck," Bonner replied. "Probably forced to walk their horses."

He turned about, stared off uptrail. "Looks like the climb gets worse."

"It does through here. But we're not too far from the top."

"The mesa — you say it's flat?"

"Fairly so. We do climb some as we double back over the highest part of the butte."

Their horses wouldn't be in very good condition for more climbing, Dave realized. Once they reached the summit the best would have gone out of them. But the outlaws' mounts would be in no better shape and likely would be much worse.

He heard the faint, distant rap of hooves in that moment, coming from far down the trail. Straining his eyes, he located the riders. There were two — not three; somebody had turned back. Either one of the horses had given out, or there was a change in plan.

"Which one?" Melinda wondered when he called her attention to the fact.

Bonner shook his head. The riders were too far down the trail to determine identity and it would be foolhardy to wait and see.

"Let's mount up," he said, turning to the horses. "Got to hold our lead."

They moved out at once, keeping their mounts to a steady walk. If they could maintain that pace, Red and Charlie Horn — it seemed to Dave that the missing man was

Sackett — would have small chance of drawing near enough to be of trouble.

Time dragged by slowly, as did the climb. Twice more they were forced to halt and rest the horses, but finally they broke out onto the summit. The first gray haze of false dawn was showing in the east and a cool breeze had sprung into life.

Dave, off the saddle quickly, walked to where he could look down on the trail. The two riders were still coming, dark shadows dogging their tracks relentlessly. He was certain now that it was Red and Horn.

They gave the horses ten minutes and moved on, now pointing due south on a wide curving course that rose to meet the horizon miles away. The trail followed a slight ridge on the mesa. It was grass covered and fairly smooth, but to the sides Bonner could see the country was rough, broken by low buttes and brush filled arroyos.

If the horses were in better condition, time and miles could be saved by slicing directly across the broad plateau, rather than holding to the circuitous trail. There was no use in considering such a plan, Dave decided; after the long, tiring climb to the top of the butte, it would be cruel to put the animals through further punishment.

He wondered if that was what had befallen

115

Sackett; had his horse simply caved in, been unable to continue? That Cal had dropped back intending to circle the butte and intercept them when they reached the crossroad mentioned by Melinda, made little sense. There were other, better places.

He became aware of Melinda; she was leaning to one side, looking down at the left front foot of her horse. She turned, and faced him.

"He's going lame," she said in a faltering voice.

Bonner halted at once. Dismounting together, they examined the hoof. There was nothing lodged in the frog and the shoe was on firm; but the black was favoring it visibly.

"We'll rest a bit," Bonner said, pulling the rifle from its boot. "Might help some."

He doubted that, but there was little else to do. "Wait here," he said. "I'll have a look at our back trail."

Wheeling, he returned to a slight knoll that offered him a good view of the land over which they had crossed. Surprise moved through him when he reached the crest of the rise; the trail was empty. Red and Charlie Horn had simply disappeared.

Bonner stood for a full ten minutes while he endeavored to locate the two men, then actually gave it up and returned to where Melinda waited. She was as worn as the horses, he noted, and greeted him with a spiritless, half smile. She was hungry — they had long since finished the scraps of jerky he had found in Horn's saddlebags — but she had voiced no complaint.

"Time to move on?" she asked, pulling herself wearily upright.

"Maybe not yet. There's nobody in sight."

Melinda frowned. "You think they turned back?"

"I'm not sure what I think. It's possible, of course. Could be they've only pulled off the road to rest."

"Were they far enough behind to lose sight —"

"They weren't that far, last time I looked. My guess is they've had to wait on the horses."

Relief crossed her drawn features. "Then we can travel slow. I doubt if my black can keep up —"

Bonner saw her eyes spread suddenly into wide circles. Her lips parted.

"Look out — Dave! Behind you —"

He was wheeling even as she cried her warning. He had a quick glimpse of the two outlaws. They were off the road, leading their horses along the sandy floor of a narrow wash. Apparently they had quit the trail, as he had considered doing, cut across country in hopes of overtaking Melinda and him. But they had miscalculated; they had overshot, blundered onto their objectives before they realized it.

At Melinda's cry, both outlaws halted. Horn reacted fast. He drew, fired and lunged to one side, all in a single motion. Bonner snapped a bullet at the man as he dived into the protection of the rocks. He knew he had missed and levered the rifle for a second try. Red, seemingly frozen momentarily, recovered and plunged hurriedly into a clump of mesquite.

"Keep down!" Dave yelled at Melinda and rushed toward the arroyo. He must stop them here and now; it could be a fatal mistake to let them escape, allow them to set up an ambush somewhere farther along the trail.

Halfway to the wash he saw motion in a clump of brush and fired point blank into it. There was no yell and he assumed he had missed again. Cursing himself, he levered a fresh cartridge into the rifle's chamber and ran on.

Almost to the edge of the arroyo, he veered left. No point in making it easy for the outlaws. Abruptly Red raised up from behind the mesquite, revolver leveled. Instantly Dave threw himself forward, went full length onto the ground as the outlaw fired. He twisted and, still moving, pressed off a shot from the rifle, levered fast and squeezed the trigger again.

There was no report, only a dull click. The weapon was empty. He heard Red yell; dropping the long gun, he rolled hard for a low mound of rocks immediately to his left. Red fired again. The bullet sent a geyser of sand spewing into Dave's face.

Bonner blinked and spat the particles from his lips as he gained the rocks. Luck had been with him on that one. A few inches higher and Red's bullet would have caught him.

Bounding to his feet, he drew his pistol, fell into a crouch. He was in between the two men he thought. Horn yelled something he did not understand, but Red's answer was clear — and close.

"Over here! Behind them rocks!"

XVIII

Dave whirled instantly and ducked low, running for the opposite side of the mound. The arroyo was five feet deep at that point and he was well above it.

He pulled up short. Charlie Horn loomed directly before him, pistol swinging up fast. Dave fired and saw the outlaw stagger as the heavy slug tore into his body, catch himself, again bring up his gun.

Horn's bullet was close and Bonner triggered a second shot. The outlaw spun half-around, sank to his knees. He struggled to lift his weapon once more, failed, began to pitch forward.

"Charlie?"

At Red's questioning shout, Bonner turned again, doubled back behind the boulders.

"Charlie — you get him?"

Red's voice sounded as though he were farther up the arroyo. Dave reached the far side of the rocks, paused, eyes probing the brush. The outlaw was not to be seen. Moving quickly, Bonner quietly dropped to the floor of the wash and hesitated.

Red was no longer shouting questions, having concluded apparently that all was not well with his partner. Bonner remained motionless for several moments while he listened into the tight hush. Red was close by; somewhere still in the arroyo. He had to be settled with.

Dave moved forward. The soft, loose sand cushioned his steps, deadened all sound. Tension was building up within him, pulling his nerves taut. Red was there, somewhere. He could be crouched behind any one of the numberless brush clumps dotting the arroyo's floor.

He froze. Something had stirred in the gray-green depths of a rabbitbush. Only a bird — one of the small horned larks so plentiful on the mesa. Bonner pressed on, taking slow, deliberate steps, pistol ready for instant use.

A sudden hammer of hooves brought him up short. He had a fleeting look at Red, bent low over his saddle, rushing out of the wash. Dave lunged to one side, threw himself flat as the outlaw fired.

The bullet dug into the bank of the wash beyond Bonner's head. He rolled to his back, sent an answering shot at the man. Red flinched, thundered on.

Alarm shot through Dave: Melinda! Red was heading straight for her. Leaping to his feet, he crossed the arroyo in long strides and heaved himself onto the bank. Red was a crouched figure bearing down on the girl.

Bonner steadied his aim with his left arm, squeezed off a bullet. It was a near miss. He saw Melinda move suddenly, and then instinctively dart behind her horse. Red fired twice in quick succession. The bullets meant for her slammed into the black, knocked him thrashing to his knees. Melinda screamed and Bonner, in a burst of rage, emptied his weapon at the outlaw and broke into a run.

He found her huddled behind the dead horse. The black had flung up his head just as Red had gotten off his shots and had taken both the slugs in his brain. Melinda was still trembling when he helped her rise.

Holding her close, Bonner stared off at the receding shape of the outlaw. Red would be ahead of them now. Could they expect more trouble — an ambush perhaps? Or was the man too badly injured to be a problem! Daylight was at hand; that would make a great difference.

He waited until Melinda had regained her composure and then pulled away gently.

"It's all over with," he said. "Red's hit — I don't think we'll see any more of him."

"And Charlie Horn?"

"Dead. We might as well start for the ranch."

She frowned. "My horse —"

"We'll use Horn's."

It was his own buckskin, he realized and, turning, walked back to the arroyo. The horse was standing behind a clump of brush. He appeared worn and was covered with sweat-caked dust, a result of the hard trip across the badlands.

But he would make it to Pitchfork and that was all that counted at the moment to Dave Bonner; get Melinda safely home. Then he would decide on his next move.

He paused long enough to retrieve Horn's pistol and belt. The odds were good that Melinda would have no use for it, but he felt it best she be armed. He explained that to her when he returned with the buckskin. She nodded and waited in silence while he reloaded the weapon. The belt was much too large for her waist, so she thrust the pistol under her skirt band and hung the belt over the horn of the saddle.

They moved out shortly after that with the sun well up and beginning its climb into a cloudless sky. It would be another hot day and neither Melinda nor the horses were in condition to face it. But they would manage somehow.

An hour later they caught sight of Red. The outlaw was a small, dark object on the horizon far ahead. He had lost all interest in them evidently, thinking now only of escape and finding someone to patch up his wound. Dave sighed with relief at that knowledge. He was having difficulty remaining awake — and fearing trouble from the outlaw kept him struggling continually to stay alert. Now he could doze in satisfaction.

Around midmorning they came out onto the brow of a low bluff and looked down onto the ranch. Dave felt his spirits lift at sight of the quiet, distant buildings surrounded by a soft blur of green grass and trees. He grinned at Melinda who smiled back.

The horses seemed to sense the nearness of journey's end also, and quickened their pace voluntarily.

"Your pa'll be plenty relieved to see you," Bonner said when they reached the floor of the valley and were starting across the long, grassy flat that led up to the rear of the barn. "Expect he's been some worried."

Melinda shrugged. "I'd never bet on it. Sometimes I think it doesn't matter to him what I do — or what happens to me."

"He just doesn't show it. I got him figured as the kind of man who never makes much fuss over anything — except on the inside."

She stared at him thoughtfully. "I'd like to believe that."

"It's most likely the truth."

She stared off toward the ranch. There was nothing visible of it now except the sprawling shape of the barn and the lines of trees fanning out from either side.

"Maybe I'll find out this time for sure. The way this is working out, Pa will have to make a choice. He'll believe Cal or he'll believe me. That is, if Cal's still around."

Bonner nodded. "You can figure on it. He left it up to Red and Horn to finish us off. He was so sure they'd do it he didn't even bother to wait for us back there where the trail joined the road. He's got too much to lose to run."

"Even if we show up?"

"It won't make any difference to him. He believes he's got the upper hand — even over your pa. He'll try bluffing his way out when we face him."

"Then you're not going after your friends, bring them back to testify?"

"Don't think I need to. I know Sackett's got my money hid out somewhere. I'll find a way to make him talk."

"With a gun?"

"If I have to. I don't like settling things that way, but sometimes there's no other answer."

He paused. The peak roofed barn was just

125

ahead. "Reckon the first thing we'd better do is find your pa, let him see that you're safe. Be good if we can sidestep Sackett."

"He may not even be here — Pa, I mean," Melinda said. "He could be out hunting you — us. It's hard to guess what kind of a story Cal told him when he got back."

"We'll wait and see," Bonner said, shifting wearily on his saddle. "No use borrowing trouble."

There was sudden motion in the underbrush at the rear of the barn. Startled, the bay shied, slammed into the buckskin as the tall figure of a man lunged abruptly into the open.

"Pull up!"

Cal Sackett's voice was high, ragged. His face was bearded, sweat-streaked; dust lay thick on his clothing. Weariness rode him like a monstrous weight and his bloodshot eyes reflected the strain under which he labored.

But the hand that held a cocked pistol was steady.

XIX

"Turn them horses around!"

At the command Bonner settled back on his saddle, allowing his arms to sink. Instantly Sackett stiffened.

"Don't get no ideas about reaching for that gun!"

Dave froze. Cal had him dead to rights — helpless. He stared at the man. There was a wildness to him. They were close to the ranch buildings and Sackett might hesitate to shoot, but he was desperate enough to do so if pushed.

Bonner raised his glance. The blank wall of the barn faced them. They would not be visible to anyone in the yard, but there could be someone inside the structure who might hear, come to investigate and distract Sackett long enough to permit him to act. Stall — that was their only hope.

"You aim to kill us both?"

Cal Sackett's eyes narrowed. "Now just what do you think?" His shoulders came forward slightly. "Where's Red and Charlie Horn?"

"Horn's dead. Red's got a bullet in him."

"Where is he?"

"Last we saw he was riding south."

"Headed for town," Sackett said in disgust. "Might've known they'd mess it up."

"They tried," Dave said and slid a glance at Melinda. She was rigid in the saddle, face pale, lips compressed to a tight line. She was looking straight ahead at the broad wall of the barn.

"You won't get away with this, Sackett," Bonner said.

"The hell I won't. I can get away with anything."

"Maybe with robbing Ed Madden — stealing his cattle, and pulling other stunts like that — but not with murdering his daughter."

"It'll be you getting the credit for that. I told him you were holding her hostage."

"He believe it?"

"Of course. He got himself a posse together and is out hunting you right now."

"That's a lie. We didn't see —"

"Sure you didn't! Think I'm loco enough to send him to the buttes? Headed him and his bunch into the brakes north of here. He thinks that's where you're holed up."

Dave nodded. "Got him out of the way while you sat back and waited for Red and Charlie Horn to do the job on us."

"It worked fine. Been setting here watching the ridge since before daylight. I knew that sooner or later Charlie and Red, or you two, would show up. If it was them, everything was all right. If it was you — then I'd have to take care of things myself."

Dave shifted his eyes to the left corner of the barn, then to the right. There was no sign of anyone. He brought his attention back to Sackett.

"Mind telling me something?"

Sackett shifted impatiently. "If you're stalling, you're wasting your time. Ain't nobody around, save the cook and a couple of stable hands. Everybody else's out on the range or with the old man."

"No reason then why I can't get the straight of this. We've got plenty of time."

"Maybe," Cal murmured. "What's eating you?"

Bonner touched Melinda with his eyes. She had turned to him and was watching closely. Apparently the girl believed he had a plan of some sort in mind; he only wished he did.

"What's this all about? I mean — why're you pulling a deal like this? The way I understand it Pitchfork will be yours someday, anyway."

"It was you — coming in here raising hell. And I'm tired of waiting. I aim to have it while I can still enjoy it — not when I'm old and stove-in like Madden. I've earned it," Sackett added in a bitter tone. "Putting up with that old bastard's yammering and being bossed. And then all the slapping around and beatings I took when I was a kid."

"He was bringing you up, like you were his own son, I hear."

"But I wasn't. She wouldn't let me forget that," Cal replied, motioning to Melinda. "Kept letting me know who and what I was. But all the time I was the one having to put up with her pa —"

"I resented that — very much," Melinda broke in, speaking for the first time.

"You was the lucky one. Maybe he was your real pa, but you had the luck. You didn't have to be with him day and night, listening to all his preaching and being ready to jump every time he hollered frog."

"I — I would have welcomed it," the girl said quietly.

Dave Bonner realized in that moment the depth of loneliness the girl had endured in those past years. Evidently Ed Madden had simply ignored her presence, had concentrated his time and effort on Cal Sackett, to appease his need for a son.

"Well, I ain't throwing it all away now," Sackett said. "Not for you or nobody else."

"You'll be throwing it away for sure if you go through with this," Dave said. "Put that gun away and we'll call it quits right here. Nothing will be said to Ed Madden by Melinda or me. You've got our promise."

Sackett wagged his head. "Ain't no use trying to sweet talk me out of it. Things've gone too far."

"Not too far to stop short of killing. You can buy us off easy — just put that gun back in your holster."

"Forget it. Like I said, I'm taking no chances on losing out."

Bonner knew he had run his course and to no avail. No one had appeared and persuading Cal to drop what he had in mind was impossible. The situation was drawing to a fine point; it would be up to him. He could see only one way out — drive his spurs into the bay, send him charging straight at Sackett and create enough diversion for Melinda to escape. He might get lucky.

"There's no need for this, Cal," Melinda said, abruptly adding her voice to Bonner's support. She had finally understood his reason for the prolonged conversation. "Why can't we run Pitchfork together? Pa's getting old. He won't be around much longer. We could team up —"

Sackett was staring at the girl. A crooked

grin pulled at his lips. "You're talking mighty friendly all of a sudden!"

"It took something like this to open my eyes, I suppose. There's no use of our being enemies — and certainly you'd be foolish to start out trying to run the ranch with two murders hanging over your head. Together we —"

"Don't hand me that!" Sackett interrupted angrily. "You ain't changed none. You're just trying to save your neck — and Bonner's. I ain't falling for no yarn like that."

"We had a lot of fun when we were kids," Melinda continued, ignoring the outburst. "We were even close, almost like brother and sister. Why can't we —"

" 'Cause too much water's run under the bridge, that's why! And you're just talking — you ain't meaning a damn thing you're saying!"

"Better listen to her, Sackett," Bonner cut in. "She's making sense. A man never stops looking over his shoulder once he's done a murder. He can't be sure he's in the clear — that somebody doesn't know about it."

"Who'd know?"

"Red, for one. He won't die from that bullet I put in him; and when they find us dead, he'll know you did it. It'll give him a club to hold over you the rest of your life."

Sackett laughed. "I can get rid of him, too."

"Maybe so. But there could be others. And Red could talk. How do you know there's not somebody hiding out there in the brush right now — watching?"

"Get them horses turned around!" Sackett yelled, suddenly out of patience. "I'm done listening to your yammering."

The moment was at hand. Dave Bonner felt his nerves go taut as he tried to calculate the instant best suited for his try. When he started to swing the bay Cal would relax his guard for an instant; during that fragment of time he would send the horse plunging head-on at the man.

He looked down at Sackett. "You aim to walk clear to the buttes?" he asked, squaring himself on the saddle. He'd go for his gun, too, when he drove home the spurs. There might be time for one shot.

"Don't worry none about me. Got a horse waiting in the brush. Move on — slow and easy. And keep your lip buttoned. I'm tired of talking."

There was a slight scraping noise at the corner of the barn. It was followed by the harsh, double click of a shotgun being cocked.

"Reckon it's my turn now," Ed Madden drawled.

XX

Cal Sackett's face went blank with surprise; and then anger narrowed his eyes, pulled at the corners of his mouth. He did not look around but instead kept his attention on Melinda and Bonner.

"You move," he said in a voice meant only for Dave, "and she's dead."

Bonner's jaw hardened. "Give it up, Sackett! He's got a scattergun pointed at your back."

"He won't use it — not on me."

Dave stared at the man. Cal was convinced he still had the upper hand, that in the eyes of the rancher he could do no wrong — even when it came down to a choice on Madden's part between him and Melinda.

Ed Madden's voice was hard. "Drop that gun!"

Sackett shook his head. "No, Pa. You ain't calling the shots this time. I know what I'm doing."

"Just what the hell are you doin'?"

"Bonner's a killer. And Melinda's mixed up in it with him. I know because —"

134

"You're a goddam liar, Cal." Madden's voice was now low, almost conversational. "Happens I heard most all that was said back here. I know what you're up to."

There was a heavy silence, broken only by the distant barking of a dog, the dry clacking of insects in the weeds.

"You hear me?" Madden demanded. "Drop that pistol you're holdin'. I ain't tellin' you again!"

Sackett relaxed slightly. "You sure this's the way you want it?"

"Damned sure. I had a hunch things wasn't just right early this mornin' when you sent me and the boys traipsin' off to the north. Then when one of them said he'd seen you and the others linin' out for Devil's Butte yesterday, I was plumb sure."

"If you'd been smart, you'd have stayed up there with that posse —"

"So I pulled out and doubled back," the rancher continued as though there had been no interruption. "I was just in time to see my daughter and that Bonner feller comin' over the ridge. When they didn't get past the barn, I come back to see why. Heard you talkin', so I just stood there and done some listenin'."

"Reckon you know how things stand then."

Ed Madden said, "Reckon so." Then in a

dragging voice, he added, "Hard to believe, Cal. I treated you like you was my own blood — maybe better. I tried to make things right for you so's you'd always have plenty. Then you up and do this to me."

"I earned everything I got!" Sackett shouted.

"I ain't sayin' you didn't. But you stood to get it all. I figured Melinda would be marryin' herself off someday, have a home of her own. Then Pitchfork would be yours — all yours. And I could rest easy, knowin' things was in good hands. But I made a mistake — a real humdinger. But I guess there ain't no way of seein' greed in a man when he's still a younker. Too bad."

"For you — old man!" Sackett yelled in a high, wild tone.

He wheeled, gun swinging fast. The early morning's hush was split by Melinda's shrill scream and the roaring blast of Madden's weapon. Cal Sackett slammed back as the charge of buckshot caught him in the belly, hurled him to the ground.

Dave Bonner dismounted slowly. He was no stranger to violence, but it had happened so swiftly that it had taken him off balance. He crossed to where Sackett lay and glanced down at the man. There was no point in checking for signs of life; no human could have survived such an onslaught. He looked up as Ed Madden halted before him.

"I had to do it," the rancher muttered. "Had to. Weren't no choice."

Dave nodded. "He would have killed you —"

Madden's eyes were on Sackett's slack face. "I just can't seem to believe it. That boy . . . was like a son."

Bonner heard Melinda move up to his side, felt her fingers upon his arm. She had gone to him — not her father. Anger stirred through him.

"You knew he was stealing you blind all the time. Why didn't you stop him?"

"Figured he was just growin' up. Doin' what most boys'll do. I didn't mind."

"You believe me now when I say he held me up — him and his bunch — robbed me of the money I was carrying?"

"I never thought he'd go that far. Ain't no reason now to doubt you."

"He admitted it," Melinda said, her voice impatient. "Cal did a lot of the things you'd never believe."

Madden raised his glance to the girl. His eyes looked old, sick, and there was a haggardness to his face.

"I'm right sorry, girl. Been tough on you, I know that. I was a plumb fool — the worst kind — because I was favorin' an outsider over my own blood. But a man's thinkin' gets sot in a groove and pretty soon he can't see nothin' else."

Melinda's attitude did not soften. It would take time, Dave knew, but eventually she would relent and forgive. Her next thought was of him.

"Your money — the cash you were carrying to buy stock for those ranchers — with Cal dead, how will you ever find it?"

It had occurred to Bonner, too. Except for Red, who might — or might not — know where the cash was hidden, his last hope for recovering had died with Sackett. He shrugged.

"This ends it, I reckon."

Ed Madden knelt over the body of Cal. "Could be packin' it," he said, laying aside the shotgun. "You have it in a belt?"

Dave nodded. The rancher pulled clear Sackett's sodden clothing. At the sight of the wound caused by the buckshot Melinda turned away, but Madden continued to probe. He shook his head.

"Ain't wearin' no money belt."

He thrust his hand into the man's pockets, drew out the odds and ends of change and other small articles he found, dumped all onto the ground in a small pile.

There were only a few dollars, nothing that

would indicate any large amount of money. Dave studied the collection, his spirits low. And then one coin suddenly caught his attention. Frowning, he stepped nearer, plucked the coin from the remainder.

It was a scarred Mexican gold piece — the one he had deposited with Sutton.

"What's that?" Madden asked, looking up.

"Good luck piece of mine," Bonner answered, his mind moving rapidly.

"Yours? Where'd Cal get it?"

"I left it with Sutton, the saloonkeeper," Dave said, thinking aloud more than in reply to the rancher's question. "I was broke when I hit town. I needed a meal and a bed. I gave it to Sutton as security for my bill."

"I ain't gettin' this," Madden said, straightening up. "If you give it to Tom Sutton how'd Cal —"

"I've got a pretty good idea how," Dave said, thrusting the coin into his pocket. Wheeling to the buckskin, he added, "And I got a good idea where that money is, too."

XXI

Grim, Dave Bonner turned into Sugarite's main street and proceeded steadily toward the Mexican Hat saloon. He looked neither right nor left, but from the corner of his eye he saw several persons halt, stare at him curiously. Among those was the town marshal.

He reached Sutton's and swung to the blind side of the building. Tieing the buckskin to a fence post, he checked his revolver, and then in quick, sure steps, mounted the porch and pushed into the darkened interior of the saloon.

Four men sat at a table to his right. Sutton, at that moment, was placing drinks before them, his back to the door. Dave moved on and, face tipped down, took up a position at the end of the bar.

Shortly, Sutton was back in his customary position. He paused to mop at a wet spot on the counter, said, "What'll it be, mister?"

Dave raised his head, brushed back his hat. "Come for that lucky piece of mine."

Sutton stiffened. His eyes widened and his mouth fell open. It was the same startled look

140

that had crossed his face that morning when Dave had stumbled into the saloon after crossing the desert. But Bonner now understood its meaning; the saloonman had thought him dead then — and now had been given that understanding for a second time.

Dave watched him squirm. "Got it handy?"

Tom Sutton swallowed hard, struggling to recover his presence of mind while he scrubbed vigorously again at the counter.

"Fact is, I don't exactly know where I put it. Take me a little while. Now, if you don't mind droppin' back —"

Dave reached into his pocket, laid the coin on the bar. "I'll save you the trouble of looking," he said. "Took it off a friend of yours — a dead friend."

Sutton stared at the coin. The sound of a chair scraping against the floor broke the hush. Bonner glanced to the backbar mirror. The four men were watching with close interest. He came back to the saloonman.

"Charlie Horn's dead, too," he said, picking up the coin and dropping it back into his pocket. "So's Skinner — and I put a bullet in Red. Could be he's with them by now."

Sutton was in a state of paralysis. He continued to stare at the spot where the coin had lain. Dave waited, allowing the information to have its full effect. Then, "It's all over,

141

friend. I want my money."

The words jarred the bar owner back to reality. "I don't know what you're talkin' about," he mumbled.

"The hell you don't!" Bonner shouted in a sudden burst of fury. "You were in with Sackett and his bunch. They left my money belt with three thousand dollars in it with you for safe keeping. I want it!"

It was a long shot, but Dave Bonner was fairly certain he was right. He watched Sutton straighten up and throw an appealing glance toward the four customers at the table.

"I don't know nothin' about it!" he declared loudly. "You got the wrong man —"

"Not much! Sackett wouldn't have been carrying that gold coin of mine if you hadn't figured I was as good as dead and given it to him!"

"No —" Sutton threw a frantic glance toward the door in the rear of the saloon as though searching for a means of escape.

Dave caught the reflection of motion in the backbar again. He spun smoothly, the heavy Colt springing into his hand in a quick blur. The men, half out of their chairs, froze.

"Stay out of this," he snarled.

The men settled back. Bonner whirled to Sutton, rested the pistol on the counter. "I waited long enough. Get my belt — and all

142

the money better be in it."

The saloonman, evidently deriving a measure of courage from the four patrons, shook his head. "I ain't got nothin' of yours."

"Don't give me that!" Dave shouted, temper again soaring. He reached out and caught Sutton by the shirt front. Yanking him up against the counter, he shoved hard and sent the man reeling into the backbar.

There was a crash of falling glasses. Dave leaned forward and picked up a half-filled bottle of whiskey, then hurled it into the mirror. The plate shattered, collapsed into a myriad of glittering splinters.

"Get it!" Dave shouted. "Get it — quick — or, by God, I'll take this place apart!"

Sprawled against the shelving, Sutton stared up at him. Bonner raised his pistol, fired. The bullet drove into the woodwork only inches from the bar owner's head.

With the thundering of the gun, there was a scurrying behind Dave. He whirled, caught only a glimpse of the four men bolting through the doorway. Smoke coiling about his head, he looked again at Sutton. The man had not stirred.

Moving around the end of the counter, Bonner halted in front of Sutton. He could hear shouting in the street. The gunshot had attracted attention and now the frightened customers were adding to the confusion. He could expect the marshal, with reinforcements, very soon.

Grasping Sutton by the arm, he dragged him to his feet, pressed him back against the bar.

"You've got about twenty seconds to hand over my money, or —" He let the sentence hang and jammed the barrel of his weapon into the man's belly.

Tom Sutton's eyes flared with pain and fear. Abruptly he sagged. Bobbing his head weakly, he said, "All right; I'll get it. In the safe," he added, pointing to a small, metal door in the lower half of the backbar. "You got to believe this, Bonner. I wasn't in on none of this — not with them. Sackett made me take it, hold it for him."

Bonner's lip curled. "Made you?"

"It's God's truth! Around here a man don't cross Cal Sackett — not if he wants to keep on livin'." He produced a key and squatted before the safe. Unlocking the door while Dave watched narrowly, he withdrew the belt and got to his feet.

"I wasn't to get none of the cash," he said. "I was only keepin' it for —"

There was a crash as the door leading to Sutton's living quarters burst open. Dave spun and caught a flashing glimpse of Red — a white bandage on his arm — leaping into the room.

Bonner fired. In that same instant he felt a bullet sear across his rib cage and realized that he and the outlaw had triggered their weapons in identical moments. He threw himself to one side, fired again. Red staggered, got off his second shot.

Tom Sutton yelled and fell back amid a clatter of glasses. Bonner leaned against the counter and tried to see through the layers of drifting smoke. Someone was shouting from the doorway, but he gave it no attention; he continued to wait and look. And then as the haze thinned he saw Red. The outlaw was sprawled, face down, on the floor.

Bonner drew himself up. A fire seemed to be raging in his side and he needed a drink. Reaching under the counter, he picked up a bottle of whiskey, pulled the cork with his teeth, and took a swallow.

"Mind tellin' me what the hell this's all about?"

At the mild, impatiently put question, Dave turned. The marshal, pistol in hand, stood on the opposite side of the bar. Beyond him a dozen of Sugarite's more curious citizens had gathered in the doorway. Dave considered the lawman wryly.

"Long story, marshal."

"I ain't carin' how long it is — I want to hear it!"

There was a disturbance at the doorway. Bonner looked up. Ed Madden and Melinda were pushing their way through the crowd. The rancher's jaw was set, but Melinda's face showed obvious relief.

"I'll do the explainin' for him, Henry," Madden said. "It's partly my fault — maybe all of it. But no mind now." He pivoted to Dave. "Appears you're a mite the worse for this. Reckon you'd better get along with my daughter there, let her fix you up."

"Not much more'n a scratch," Bonner said, moving out from behind the bar. "I'd like to talk some business with —"

"Time enough for that later!" Madden snapped testily. "Do what I'm tellin' you. Melinda'll take you in the buggy. I'll bring your horse."

"Yessir," Dave said, grinning, and turned to the waiting girl.

XXII

The herd had already moved out, being driven by three riders Ed Madden had lent him for the trip to Ocotillo Flats. He had made a good deal with the rancher and Bonner knew the men he represented would be more than pleased.

Standing beside the buckskin, ready to mount and ride, he faced Melinda and her father. They were on the steps fronting the porch.

"I'm obliged to you," he said, feeling a strange reluctance to depart. "Buying stock at the price you quoted me will be a big help to us all."

Madden stirred. He was looking at Melinda, his lined face pulled into a frown. In the two days that had elapsed since the death of Cal Sackett they had drawn closer.

"I'm the one that's beholden," he said. He moved off the lower step to the ground's level. "Dave, I've been tryin' to say somethin' to you the whole dang day."

Bonner studied the older man. "Say it."

"Well — way things ended up, I'm in a

147

powerful bad need of a good foreman. Gettin' too old myself to look after things, proper like. I was wonderin' — you be interested sellin' that place of yours and takin' over the job?"

The rancher paused, nodded to Melinda. "Know my pardner'd be all for it."

Dave glanced at the girl. Her eyes were bright with hope and there was a smile on her lips. The reluctance within him strengthened. It was hard to think of a future without Melinda — and the idea of running a vast spread such as Pitchfork. But after a moment he shook his head.

"I appreciate the offer, but I reckon not. I got a pretty good start on my place and I like the Ocotillo country. I sort of want to be there, watch it grow — be a part of it."

Melinda lowered her head. Quickly Ed Madden said, "I'd sure make it worth your while. And I'll treat you right."

"Know you would, but like I said, I figure I'm better off working my own range. Only thing — I got to admit it's plenty lonesome down there. I could use a partner of my own — a wife, maybe."

Melinda's head came up slowly. Her lips parted in a smile. "Dave Bonner — is this your idea of a proposal?"

He shifted awkwardly. "I've been wanting

to ask. I just wasn't sure you'd listen."

"What the hell's wrong with you?" Madden demanded gruffly. "You plumb blind? The girl's been moonin' around for days!"

Bonner squared his shoulders. "Then I'm asking straight out — will you marry me, Melinda?"

She came off the porch and into his arms in a rush. "Oh, Dave — you know I will!"

"When?"

"Whenever you say —"

"What's wrong with right now?" Ed Madden wanted to know. "Ain't nothin' like gettin' things done."

She turned to her father. "Will it be all right, Pa? Leaving you, I mean . . ."

" 'Course it'll be all right!"

"Then let's make it today," Dave said, a warm glow possessing him. Not only was he returning to the Flats with a fine herd of cattle, but he had also found the woman he had always hoped for.

"Good," Madden said in a decisive way. "We'll ride into town, look up the preacher and get the marryin' done. I expect that calls for a weddin' present on my part. Five hundred head of prime stock be all right?"

Dave Bonner frowned. "No need for you —"

Melinda placed her fingers against his lips. "Please. Let him do it," she murmured. "He wants to — well — sort of make up for things."

Bonner nodded and smiled. He guessed he was one of the lucky ones.

Ray Hogan is an author who has inspired a loyal following over the years since he published his first Western novel EX-MARSHAL in 1956. Hogan was born in Willow Springs, Missouri, where his father was town marshal. At five the Hogan family moved to Albuquerque where Ray Hogan still lives in the foothills of the Sandia and Manzano mountains. His father was on the Albuquerque police force and, in later years, owned the Overland Hotel. It was while listening to his father and other old-timers tell tales from the past that Ray was inspired to recast these tales in fiction. From the beginning he did exhaustive research into the history and the people of the Old West and the walls of his study are lined with various firearms, spurs, pictures, books, and memorabilia, about all of which he can talk in dramatic detail. Among his most popular works are the series of books about Shawn Starbuck, a searcher in quest for a lost brother who has a clear sense of right and wrong and who is willing to stand up and be counted when it is a question of fairness or justice. His other major series is about lawman John Rye whose reputation has earned him the sobriquet The Doomsday

Marshal. "I've attempted to capture the courage and bravery of those men and women that lived out West and the dangers and problems they had to overcome," Hogan once remarked. If his lawmen protagonists seem sometimes larger than life, it is because they are men of integrity, heroes who through grit of character and common sense are able to overcome the obstacles they encounter despite often overwhelming odds. This same grit of character can also be found in Hogan's heroines and in THE VENGEANCE OF FORTUNA WEST Hogan wrote a gripping and totally believable account of a woman who takes up the badge and tracks the men who killed her lawman husband by ambush. No less intriguing in her way is Nellie Dupray, convicted of rustling in THE GLORY TRAIL. Above all, what is most impressive about Hogan's Western novels is the consistent quality with which each is crafted, the compelling depth of his characters, and his ability to juxtapose the complexities of human conflict into narratives always as intensely interesting as they are emotionally involving.